UNSPOKEN SERIES

BOOK II

FINDING HOME

Written by
A. K. Moss

Other books by A. K. Moss

Unspoken book 1 in Series 2014

Cowhorse in the Making poetry 1999

Cowgirl in the Making poetry 1998

Cowboy in the Making 1998

FINDING HOME

BOOK II in

UNSPOKEN SERIES

A.K. MOSS

As long as we allow the horse to search for his strength and confidence, it will remind us to keep searching for ours.

– A.K. Moss

Books cover design by www.angelheartdesign.org

Book Cover Art by www.lauriehueckmanart.com

Book interior by RedRaven   www.redravendp.blogspot.pt

ISBN - 978-1514783955

This book is dedicated to Billie Flick. Thank you for being a true friend and listening to the layout as seventy-two hours began a great adventure and a wonderful story. And to all the horses that touched my life, who allowed me to make mistakes and guided me without judgment yet made me toe the line. I still have much to learn.

Courage is the most important of all the virtues because without courage you can't practice any other virtue consistently.

– Maya Angelou

1

Ben looked over the top of his glasses. His whiney voice seemed to pierce Paige's eardrums. "You signed on to be a temporary foster parent for this child," he said.

"All she does is sit in the house and stare at the walls," Paige countered as she glared back at the caseworker. "I'm up to here." She raised her hand to just below her eyes. "I can't force her to want to live."

"Give her more time," Ben said, his eyes showing the exhaustion of listening to complaining foster families. His life was filled with unwanted children, complaining foster parents, and natural parents who were too busy to utilize visitation privileges. Then there were the regulations that any sane man would burn. After eighteen years working with the system, he had heard it all, seen it all, and become numb. All he wanted to do was keep the girl where he had her until he could find yet another home for her. Paige had to keep Abigail; no one else wanted the girl.

"Her parents have been dead almost six months," he repeated to her, hoping to renew her sympathy. "Her whole life has been turned upside down."

Paige was venting, she couldn't get the girl to eat or drink. She wouldn't speak. Paige felt exasperated and helpless. It wasn't supposed to be this way. One moment she was a single woman trying to make a living and the next thing she knew she agreed to bring a temporary foster child in, one who hated everyone and everything. "I am at a loss here, Ben. I don't know what to do with her." Her voice was shaking.

"We can give her antidepressants. And if you need, Paige, we can give you something for your stress," the caseworker replied. "I can call and get you a prescription."

"No! That ain't it. I don't want drugs. I just want my life back."

"I can't really help you out with that until we find another foster care facility."

"I know." Paige sighed. "I am just frustrated. I have tried everything I know to get her to open up. I just don't know what to do." Paige thought for a moment about what the girl had been through.

***

Abigail Sorenson was a free-spirited girl, born to an older couple who gave her what she wanted most of the time. When preparing to go on vacation, she thought if she threw a temper tantrum, it would change their minds. But it didn't. She hadn't wanted to go.

"Now honey," her mother had said in her sweetest voice, "this will be fun. We will travel in the car and see Hells Canyon and other amazing places."

Abigail was seething, sitting in the backseat of the car with music blaring in her ear buds. Not what she called fun. Her life was filled with shopping malls, nice clothes, the Internet, and a smart phone that made all of her friends envious. Anything in life of any importance was at the touch of a finger. Then on that particular day going through the desert, no service, no iTunes, nothing but silence and her parents sitting up front acting like they were having fun. She wanted to make them as miserable as she was.

A sunny day, a winding road, and a speeding car coming around a corner too fast resulted in a head-on collision. Both of her parents were killed instantly. Abigail was pinned in the backseat with both of her legs smashed. With months of physical therapy ahead of her and the news of her parents, Abigail's life disintegrated before her eyes and sent her into a downward spiral of depression and anger.

It seemed that everyone was telling her what to do, what she couldn't do, how she should feel, how not to feel, and how not to hide her feelings. How was she supposed to do all that when she didn't know what feeling she had? She just felt alone, isolated and very angry. She buried herself even deeper into a life of electronics and Internet—a world where she didn't have to try to please anyone and she could be whoever she wanted. The person she was chatting with on the other end would never know that she was a cripple.

The first two foster homes didn't know what to do with her anger. Throwing tantrums like never before, within two to three weeks they would pull up to the DHS and say, "We just wanted to help that poor child. But we don't need to put up with this."

Abigail had taken a vase at her last foster home and thrown it across the room when her so-called foster mother told her she needed to get up and help around the house.

"Can't you see I'm crippled? My legs don't want to work," Abby had puked back at her, her voice seething with rage.

"I won't have it," the foster mother had said to Ben. She returned Abigail to the DHS office with her clothes packed and her few belongings in a box. "She is an ungrateful brat!" the woman had said under her breath as she set down the belongings then walked out the door, got in her car, and left. The woman never looked back.

Abigail looked at Ben. Her whole life had been removed from her except a box. A box with a few pictures, a couple of knickknacks from her mother, a radio, and a few other odds and ends carelessly tossed on the floor. This was her life? She looked to him for answers but it came out as sarcasm. "Now what?" she said as if it wasn't a question but more of a statement. Was he going to give up on her too?

***

How did Paige get caught up in this? Ah yes, a phone call from a friend of a friend of a friend… Paige didn't know much about the girl, and Ben had kept the description of her to a bare minimum. Now here Abigail Sorenson was, a temporary foster child until a more suitable home could be found.

The first couple of days Abigail was quiet and withdrawn. Paige figured maybe a couple of weeks of having company would be alright and it would be nice to share a little bit of her life with a young girl. By the third day, the honeymoon was over. Abigail didn't like the silence of the ranch. She didn't like the horses or the border collie cross that Paige called Blue.

The dog just sat there staring at Abigail with her ghost ice blue eyes when Paige was not in the house. It was almost like the dog was looking right through her, peering into her soul. Abigail didn't like that. She was not going to get close to anything ever again. Nothing.

Abigail raised her crutch as if to strike Blue. "Git!" she spat under her breath.

Blue got up and walked away, turned around two or three times then laid down between the kitchen and the front room door. She was definitely out of striking distance. She faced Abigail and sighed then lay there as if she was waiting for something.

Stupid dog, what are you waiting for? Abigail wondered. *I ain't going anywhere.*

The sun shone into the window giving a golden look to the peach walls that warmed the place. Abigail didn't want sun, she didn't want light, she didn't want happiness. She wanted to die. She wanted her old life. A tear rolled down her cheek. No TV, no Internet, no outside world. Just that damned dog and the horses outside that nickered every time anyone walked out the door just because their greedy little mouths wanted to be fed.

Paige had wanted Abigail to go with her this morning, but like always, Abigail said no before the words were out of Paige's mouth. Abigail pulled the blinds and sat in the house in the silence, the dead silence. Usually Blue would go with Paige, but this morning Blue was worried and paced by the fence going down toward the spring.

"No, Blue, not now. We will go down later." Paige ruffled her head and scruffed her neck. Blue always loved to go down to the spring and play in the water. There was a place at the spring that was a mucky bog of rotten vegetation and seemed a bottomless pit of mud. In the spring Paige would bring a couple of buckets of it to put on her garden. It was the best fertilizer. Blue looked again toward the spring then resigned to laying down and waiting.

"Abby, I will be back in a couple of hours. Looks like Blue will stay with you."

"Whatever," was the reply.

What was Paige supposed to do with that? A girl locked away in a house so far from living, from being, and so distant it seemed as if nothing would ever reach her.

Now here Paige was in the Department of Human Services talking with a caseworker.

Ben's whiney voice persisted, "Paige, you need to bring her in so we can evaluate her and make sure she is not suicidal. We need to determine whether she needs any meds to get over this depression. We have another six weeks of therapy scheduled to see if we can make any progress. I will have Dr. Marks evaluate her when she comes in." Ben thumbed through another file on his desk.

"I don't think she needs more therapy," Paige said. "I think she needs a reason."

"A reason for what?" he challenged, his educated eyes looking over his glasses, questioning her emotional state. From where he sat, he knew by experience that there was a name for every emotion and a pill to bring that emotion out. His goal was to find people that would take in kids and get them to be socially acceptable. If it couldn't be on their own accord or through counseling, then with the help of doctors. It seemed that pills were the answers to all his prayers—just give them a few so they get their feelings under control.

She looked at him as he repeated again, "A reason for what? Ms. Cason?"

"A reason to live," she replied quietly, then got up and walked out of his office.

2

Abigail used her crutches to get outside. She felt penned up and irritated. She just couldn't figure it out. Paige was supposed to be pushing her to exercise, but she wasn't. Abigail was supposed to be walking and strengthening her legs, working on getting the mobility back, but Paige never pushed her. Why not? She was sick of sitting in the house. The walls felt like they were closing in on her, but she sure wasn't going into town to be evaluated again and have someone tell her what they thought was in her best interest. She didn't want to see anyone, especially the caseworker. She couldn't stand him.

Paige can go by herself. She is the one who wanted me to live here, she thought. Abigail felt restless. She needed to do something, so she decided to walk down to the spring where the ground was fairly flat, which made it easy for her to maneuver her crutches. Blue followed her to the gate. Abigail looked at the closed gate then back at the dog.

"No, you stay here," Abby said sternly. Blue looked at her and then back at the gate. "I said, you stay here," Abigail repeated.

Blue dropped her head and whined. Then she trotted to the corner of the yard, looked in the direction of the spring, and barked.

Abby went out the gate and latched it before Blue came back. "You are going to stay here. I don't want you to get all wet and yucky at the spring." Her voice was softer.

Blue looked helpless. She put her paws on the gate and looked at Abigail again, then barked twice.

"I will be back in a few minutes." For the first time since Abigail had been at Paige's house, she reached through the fence and stroked Blue's head for a moment. Blue looked at her with intense eyes and whined.

Abigail turned and began to make her way down to the spring. It was a clear, beautiful day and a breeze teased and wrestled with her auburn hair. She focused on her crutches and her footing. She made it through the pasture gate and closed it behind her. There was a small clump of trees to her left and the grass was long and dry, so she had to make sure she stayed on the path.

She let her mind wander to what life would be like if things were different. If she still had her parents, she would be at home with her cell phone, playing games, daring her friends to do things they shouldn't. Life would be safe and unchanged, but it wasn't. Her life had changed, and no matter how much she fought it, the wind still blew, the grass still waved and the spring water still rolled through the curves and crevices that lined the banks, drawn by a force in silent motion.

Abigail saw a small twig in the water and watched it flow with the current. It got tangled in some grass at the edge of the ditch for a moment, did a few circles, then continued on its journey. It tumbled over rocks then flowed around the bend bobbing with the current. All of the sudden she had a thought. *Life was like this spring, forever moving forward, not stopping for anything, yet it had turns and twists and things it ran into but always kept flowing. If you get hung up, you have to figure out how to let go and move on.*

A cry came from the spring outlet where the water seeped from the depths of the ground to reach sunlight and air. Then there was silence and only the breeze playing with the tall grass. *Was that a puppy or a kitten?* she wondered. *Or maybe just my imagination running wild. Nope, there it was again.* It sounded like something was hurt. Abby bit her lower lip in concentration, then lifting her crutches, she placed them carefully on the narrow path that lay before her. She hobbled toward the sound around the bend. What she saw made her stop stone cold.

There laying in the boggy mud of the spring was a baby colt, his little blazed head about two feet from solid ground. He left imprints in the mud where he had been banging it with the effort of trying to get out. His nose stuck out in hopes of reaching solid ground, and his little nostrils flared with anxiety and effort. His eyes almost closed. Half of his little body was hidden by mud, his sides heaving from exhaustion.

Out of the corner of her eye, Abigail saw a movement, something golden, a cougar, moving stealthily through the grass—silent, focused, and circling the baby. She had seen pictures of them but never a real one. Abigail eased forward for a better look. A grouse flew out from the tall grass next to where she had put her crutch, and she jumped, startled by the beat of wings. She felt a twinge of pain from the pressure of her crippled leg and she froze. She had to ignore it. Not more than thirty feet from her, the cougar cocked an ear in her direction and brought her to reality.

What should she do? Her heart was in her throat. The cougar hissed, and then the sound of purring resonated in the still air.

The baby lifted his exhausted head and squealed with effort. One front leg lifted out of the mud and bent at the knee. He held it out of the hole, rested a moment, then tried to get the second front leg up. He banged his little head in the mud again. Abigail heard the suction of mud attempting to hold its grip. The cat paced back and forth in front of the baby. Again he struggled and moved a couple more inches. The mud was losing its grip.

The cougar walked by the baby's head reached out its paw to test the mud, then crept toward the nose of the baby as if playing with its new toy. It touched the colt's nose gently with the pad of its large paw. The baby screamed again, hoping in vain that his mama would come and save him. He tried to turn his body in an attempt to stay outside the reach of the cat. The mud released his other front leg, and his sharp little hooves reached more solid ground. He lurched forward, but his hind legs were still mired in the muddy tomb of the spring.

The cat hissed again. It seemed to know the baby was almost out and watched patiently. The colt struggled again, his sides heaving and giving another lurch forward. His hind end moved a little. As if that was a signal for the cougar, the cat crouched down behind the colt's neck. It stayed stock-still. The only thing moving was the tip of its tail twitching back and forth; the cat had played this waiting game before. The colt turned a little more and had his shoulders completely out of the mud. The cat was ready to make a spring at him. And just as it went to leap at the colt's neck…

Abigail screamed without thought. She took her crutches and banged them on a tree, then started to hobble toward the downed colt. The shock of the sudden noise made the cougar jump straight in the air as if it had been shot. It made three leaps toward the safety of a tree and froze, looking for the threat and not wanting to give up on such an easy catch of colt meat. The colt, also surprised, gave a sudden surge, his exhausted legs shaking as he squealed with all his effort and moved another five or six inches.

Abigail knew he was going to make it. The colt could get out with a little help. Abigail had to move fast, but with her crippled leg, she really needed to use her head. She reached down, grabbed a couple of rocks and started throwing them at the cat. The cat hissed. Abby took her sweatshirt off as she dropped her crutches and started swinging it over her head and making all kinds of screechy war whoop types sounds. She grabbed one of her crutches and banged the branches overhead making the cat look up while she threw more rocks. Keeping the cat busy so as not to focus on the colt, Abigail flung the sweatshirt up in the air again holding on to one sleeve. The cat couldn't take any more of the crazy girl screeching and howling. It took off down through the trees, silently disappearing.

The colt lay silent as if accepting his fate or playing dead. The only parts of him that moved were his sides heaving in the mid-morning sun. Abigail had to do something fast. The house was over a hundred yards away. She had no experience with cougars but knew the cat would be back. It wouldn't go far. She had to save that baby. Abigail started toward the colt. It lifted its head, saw her, and nickered pleadingly.

Abby forgot her leg. She forgot her parents and the life she had lost. She only focused on the baby. She hobbled up toward the baby's head and talked to it.

"Easy, big guy, easy," she coaxed him. "I am gonna get you out of here, alright?"

Her mind was racing. What could she do? She reached out to touch his nose, and the colt reached out to smell her. In another attempt to find some ground with his hind legs, he surged forward again. Abby had to move to the side so he wouldn't bump into her.

With her sweatshirt still in hand, she tested the mud where the colt's front feet were. It was fairly firm and held her weight pretty well. She then brought her sweatshirt slowly out along the mud and reached toward the colt's neck. She rubbed him with it a few times then brought the sleeve over the baby's neck, rubbing and talking all the while. The baby's ears twitched and listened to her shaky voice. Abigail adjusted her hands to get a firm hold on the sweatshirt. She leaned back and gave a tug while the baby threw back his head. With the leverage of the sweatshirt pulling to the side, the suction of the mud released its hold. The colt toppled forward—attempting to find his footing again—and with shaky legs, he stood on solid, damp ground. Abigail fell sideways and landed in the mud. The sticky goo clung to her as she rolled over to pull herself out.

Abigail heard another hiss. She swung her head around as panic filled her heart. There was no way to save the baby now. She could hardly move in the mired muck she had fallen into. Blue burst through the dried grass at top speed. The dog passed the colt and the girl and ran straight for the camouflaged feline. Blue barked with every stride, gaining ground and hot on the trail of a disappointed, hungry cat.

Abigail reached for dried grass where she could get a hold and help pull her out of the mud. She crawled to her fallen crutches and clamored the best she could to get upright. The colt just stood there, shivering and swaying back and forth. Abigail talked to him. "It's alright, big guy." She touched him on the neck, and he bobbed his head, his little legs shaking with weakness. He couldn't be more than a couple of weeks old. "Where is your mama?" Abigail asked as she took her hand and scooped off more mud from the side of her newfound friend.

She didn't know how she was going to get him to the house. She thought of leaving him there, but then what if he wandered off. How would she find him again in the tall grass?

She thought of leading him with her sweatshirt, but it was laying there in the mud—and she sure wasn't going back in there. So she decided to try and just coax him along. She tried to push him in the direction of the house. He just swayed trying to keep his feet. Then she tried to sweet talk him. "Come on, baby, you can come with me." She walked toward him, but he just looked disheartened. As she passed him, his shaky legs started to move in stumbling steps to follow her as she walked away. Subconsciously he put one foot in front of the other, and with eyes half closed, he followed by instinct.

Abigail thought she heard the cat hiss from behind her, and her heart leapt into her throat. She searched through the tall grass for any sign of haunting yellow eyes, but instead she saw the head of Blue coming from a good chase, panting happily.

"Blue!" she said as she hobbled on her crutches. "You about scared me to death."

Blue looked at her and wiggled her dock-tailed butt. She circled around Abigail, but she would not leave the girl's side. Abigail looked around, feeling a bit more courage now that Blue was there. She reached down, feeling the security of the dog and stroked her soft head.

She had to keep moving. "Come on, cougar, you want a fight? We will give you a fight. Huh, Blue?" she said under her breath. She hobbled a little faster, "Cougar." Hmmm, she'd found a name for her friend.

"Come on, Cougar," she repeated. Her stride was more deliberate, her awareness of her surroundings had increased, and she moved with much more confidence. She was alive. "Gotta keep going," she said to Cougar. His little head bobbed in time with his legs as he tried to keep up with her.

About half way there, she stopped for a moment to give them all a break. Abigail reached down and stroked Blue's head. "You are a good girl, huh? That is why Paige likes you around." Blue wiggled her butt again. Abigail looked at her. "You're a wiggle butt. That is what you are. A wiggle butt." Blue lifted her upper lips as if to smile and looked at her with ghostly pale eyes.

As Abigail closed the gate to the spring pasture, she had to think about what to do with the baby. As she walked toward the barn, she thought of the stalls there. They had fresh sawdust and were clean, so with little effort, Cougar followed her into the smallest stall. Abby looked at the helpless baby, and her heart ached for him. Tears streaked her face. What was she going to do?

She crutched her way to the house to call Paige. What was she going to say? Guess she would figure that out when she started talking. She sat down and put her leg up. It was throbbing. But that baby needed something, and Abigail didn't know what it would be. She dialed Paige's cell number.

3

Craig Curry was almost off shift. It was the anniversary of his wife's death. He tried not to think of that day, but it penetrated his mind. Having been married for almost two years, his wife five months pregnant with their first baby, life couldn't have seemed sweeter. During a quiet Sunday afternoon drive along the back roads of New York, he handed her two airline tickets to Oregon. She was going to meet his dad after the baby was born and was able to travel. He remembered her smiling at him as she looked at the tickets.

"Do we have to wait a whole year?" she asked.

"Yep, by that time the kid will be up and moving around a little. And I just put in for my vacation for that time. I can't wait for you to meet him, Lisa. He is going to love you," Craig remembered saying.

He had stopped at the stoplight, and they were both quiet in the solitude, thinking of the future. When the light turned green, Craig paused a moment before pulling out into the intersection. He never looked and neither one of them saw the dump truck coming. Craig heard the brakes of the big truck, but all he saw was the grill coming straight through the passenger side. The impact was so hard it threw his little car down the street. He remembered feeling like he was floating, then something against his leg—his wife thrown next to him, her eyes wide with fright, looking at him. But no breath came from her mouth, her eyes didn't blink, and blood ran from a gash to her head. Not running but gushing. He reached for her to try to stop the blood. He hollered at her. "Nooooo!" It seemed as if someone else was saying it. He heard the words but he didn't recognize his own voice.

Someone was reaching inside to get him out. They got his door open, grabbing his arm, pulling, pulling. Still he could not let go of her.

"Lissssaaaa! Noooo!" He heard the scream again. Then the words went from his mouth to his brain.

"Hey, Mister, you got to get out. Are you alright? Oh God, call 9-1-1. Somebody get an ambulance." These words Craig heard but everything seemed to be a blur.

Craig was numb, he couldn't move, he couldn't resist the tugging and pulling of his body. The smell of hot radiator fluid and gasoline was making him gag, and he felt the heat of the engine. Sirens started ringing in his ears, and he felt himself being lifted from the car, laid out on a gurney, the straps and neck brace put in place. But none of it made any sense. He could hear the Jaws of Life working at extracting the door from the passenger side. His family and future were pulled from his life and taken away. There was no way humanly possible to hold her, to reach her, to see her smiling at him. All gone, never to feel her again.

As a New York police officer, he was supposed to be trained in these situations. He was supposed to know what to do. Helplessness filled his heart. He closed his eyes, then opened them again. Was there a chance she would be alright? Maybe this was just a dream. The gurney rolled toward the ambulance, and the medics were giving orders and reading vitals on him. His mind was numb. He felt a bump and a shove as they loaded him in the ambulance. Wasn't he the one who was supposed to save people? Wasn't he the one who was supposed to be strong and protect his wife? How could he not have looked both ways? How could he have been so stupid giving her tickets a year in advance? He would not have been daydreaming when he should have been driving.

***

The radio went off in the cop car and brought Craig back to reality. He shifted in his seat to shake the memories' hold on him and listened to the call. He had two more hours before he was off shift. He had been back on the force for the last eight months. It was good to be active and working, having situations put in front of him that he had to find solutions for. Having people who needed help that he could support or cuffing someone who was out of hand and needed a little "time out" in a cell, as he called it, sometimes would do the trick. Then there was the darker side of his job. He wouldn't go there, not today. People did what they did, and he had no control over it. He had taken an oath, he was there to protect and serve.

It had been a pretty easy day, and he was looking forward to maybe having a beer at the end of the shift. This call was a bad one, and it was in their jurisdiction.

They had a hostage situation. A man had his son held at gunpoint in his house. The mother had called 9-1-1 and was frantic. Apparently, the man had lost his job that day and gone off the deep end.

Craig's partner, John, answered the call. "We are on our way."

"Well, let's see what we can do," Craig said as he pulled out. "This doesn't sound good though."

They wouldn't take the conversation any further than that. They drove in silence with lights flashing.

Craig parked the car about half a block from the house. They quietly got out and started to case the perimeter and windows to assess the situation. Craig looked inside the picture window and saw the man holding a gun to his son's head.

The man and the boy were both sobbing. "I have to do it. I have to." He was looking at his wife.

Before Craig could even get a word out, the man raised the gun, shot his wife, his son, and himself in rapid succession. All three lay motionless.

Craig fell to his knees, holding his head. He closed his eyes and told himself, "I didn't see what I just saw. Please, God, I didn't see what I just saw." He opened his eyes and looked inside the window. Instinct kicked in, he felt his body in motion moving toward the door like he was in a trance. "Save the boy, save the wife, save them," he repeated to himself.

Craig heard John's voice speaking into the radio, "Shots fired. Repeat, shots fired. Send ambulance!"

4

John stopped at Craig's apartment. It had been a week since the shooting. Craig hadn't taken it so well and was having a hard time getting back into the role of protect and serve.

John's stout frame stood in the doorway. "Come on, Craig. Let's go out and have a beer."

"No, I don't think so. I have whiskey right here." He reached into his cupboard and pulled out a bottle of Crown Royal. "This was my dad's favorite. Goes down smooth and warms an ice cold heart." He pulled off the velvet pouch that protected the gold liquid.

"Well then, looks like we can stay right here," John stated with a smile. "Do you have any steaks to cook?"

"Yeah, got a couple in the freezer, help yourself."

John took them out and threw them into the microwave. "What else you got?" He searched through the cupboards. They were mainly bare. "Not looking too promising," he warned in a teasing voice.

"I got a couple of potatoes in the fridge," Craig answered as he poured a shot in each glass.

John opened the fridge. There was a carton of sour milk, some eggs, withered carrots, and soggy tomatoes. He found the potatoes and gladly closed the door.

The apartment was dusty and old looking. The walls were a pale blue, and the tan carpet needed vacuuming. Other than that, the dishes were done and the table was cleared off. John walked out onto the balcony and poured briquettes in the barbeque grill. He poured starter fluid over the top of them, waited a second, pulled out a match, and struck it. As it flared up, he dropped it in and watched the flames come to life. He left the glass door open to allow a little breeze to flow through the stale air of the apartment.

John sat down with his drink. The afternoon sun filtered in through the window, and the busy street down below seemed to give no rest to his friend. A car honked, kids screamed down the hallway of the apartment building, and somebody hollered from the sidewalk.

Craig came and sat with him and said, "Do you ever wonder what life would be like if things were handled differently?"

"Sure, I wonder that all the time, Craig, but I don't know how to change it. What are you thinking?"

"Oh, I don't know," Craig hesitated. "I was just thinking of when I was a kid."

"Yeah, you were raised in Oregon, right?"

"Eastern Oregon to be exact."

"Oh, is that something like North Carolina and South Carolina?" John grinned at his little joke.

"I don't know. The west side is pretty crowded. I like the east side a little better." Craig sighed. "It is more like freedom and openness. Like stepping up on a horse and riding for several miles before you run into someone." He thought of gathering cows with his dad. "It is more about silence and hearing yourself think, I guess." He paused. "I don't know, I am just thinking out loud." He took a sip of Crown. "I guess it has to do with a little bit of self-reliance maybe. Being responsible for yourself and what you have."

"I don't know what that is like." John looked at his friend. He knew the traffic light had changed as the cars were starting to move and shift. Everyone was in a hurry to get to the next light so they could wait there. "I have never been there, Craig. I have never been anywhere but here. What brought you here anyway?"

"I moved here with my mother when I was sixteen. Left the ranch life, my horses and even my cowboy hat behind—everything I loved at the time was left on Oregon soil." He thought for a moment, "I went to school here. Mom shifted all of my extracurricular activities to things she thought were important. She wanted me to experience life, she said. It will be fun, she said." He threw his right hand up in the air to imitate her.

"I guess she thought life was champagne and operas. She was pretty frustrated with me when I took up karate and self-defense. I had a couple of my classmates get beat up pretty bad in school, so I thought I wanted to become a cop after I graduated. And now here I am. Got married to Lisa…" Craig's voice faded off. "Now I am a widower cop at age twenty-five. I wonder how much of life she wants me to experience."

John listened. He never knew Craig's story. He had been his partner for the last three years, been through his wife's death, yet had never taken the time to hear what took place before Lisa and his marriage. John leaned back in his chair and crossed his legs.

"What did your mom think of you becoming a cop?"

John asked with interest.

"She was furious. She said *that if I wanted to waste my life, I could have just gone and lived with my father.*" Craig mimicked his mom as best as he could. "That was what I wanted to do in the first place." His voice trailed off again. "But Lisa loved New York. She loved the fast pace and the friends here. She didn't want to move to Oregon. And I wanted Lisa. She was the best thing that happened to me since I moved here." Craig thought for a moment and gave a half laugh, more out of sadness than out of humor. "I had bought tickets to take her over to meet my dad a year ago this month. We wanted the baby to be old enough to travel, and she would probably be almost walking now. Dad would have loved being a Grandpa, I think." Craig paused again then continued, "He flew out for their funeral and we had a good father-son talk, then he headed back to the ranch." Craig ran his finger around the rim of his glass and took another sip of whiskey.

"Do you still have the tickets?" John asked.

"Huh?" Craig asked dreamily.

"The airline tickets, when were you going to travel to Oregon?"

"Oh, I don't know, this month sometime," Craig answered halfheartedly. "I haven't even thought about them in so long. It really doesn't matter."

"The hell it doesn't," John shot back excitedly. "Where did you put them? Are they still good?"

"I guess they would be. They would be in my top drawer." Craig got up from the table and headed to the bedroom. He opened the top drawer and in the bottom tucked way under some pictures were the two airline tickets.

He looked at them for a moment, read Lisa's name, and ran his fingers over the spelling. He saw her smile and felt a fresh breeze come through the window. He looked at the date—*the twenty-fourth*. He thought for a moment, *Today is the twentieth.*

John went out and put steaks on the grill.

Craig came back from the bedroom with the tickets in his hand. "Looks like I will be going home."

5

Paige was at the grocery store picking up a few things. Her cell phone started to ring. She debated whether to answer it. *Dang thing*, she thought, then pulled it out of her jeans' pocket. It was Abigail.

She answered it. "Hey, Abbs, what's up?" Paige listened and in half a stride stopped short. "What did you find? Where is it now? Are you alright? Ok. Ok." Paige's mind was racing on what needed to be done. "Listen to me, Abby. I need you to get some warm water and a syringe out of the barn. It is in the tack room in a drawer. That baby is in shock. He needs water. I want you to fill the syringe and squirt it in his mouth. Keep him drinking warm water and keep rubbing him. I will be out there as soon as I can. See you in a bit."

Paige got off the phone and dialed the vet clinic. "This is Paige Cason. I have a baby colt out at the house that sounds like he is in shock. Can you send someone out there right away to take a look at him?" She paused. "Perfect. See you there."

She put her cell phone back in her pocket and headed down the aisle. When she got up to the checkout counter with her groceries, she noticed there was one checker and six people in line. She left her half-full cart and headed home.

When she pulled her '76 Chevy pickup into the driveway, spraying up gravel, she hollered for Abby.

"Down here!" Abigail called out from the barn.

Paige jogged down into the dim light of the stall in the corner. "How is he doing?" Paige asked as she opened a wood window on the outside wall of the barn to let a little light in the corner.

She saw a muddy mess of a baby palomino colt lying flat out in the sawdust.

"I don't know," Abigail replied. "He is just laying here." She was rubbing him with a towel. Tears had streaked down her face as she looked at the shivering body of the colt.

"Has he drank any water?"

Helplessly Abigail looked up. "Some, but I don't know for sure how to get it in him."

"Well let's see if we can help him get some more," Paige said confidently.

Paige tested the water. It was still warm. She filled the syringe, lifted his head, put it in his cheek, and slowly squirted it into his mouth. He swallowed. "Good boy," Paige said as she rubbed underneath his jaw line. His head was heavy and lifeless, but he subconsciously swallowed again as Paige squirted more into his cheeks back behind the tongue.

"Abbs, can you go and get me a blanket? We need to get him warm."

"Sure," Abigail said. She looked around for a moment then crutched her way to the house and got the blanket off her bed. She wrapped it around her shoulders and noticed the mud on her arms. She would deal with the dirt later. She walked out the bedroom door back down to the barn. She carefully draped the blanket over the baby.

"Come on, Cougar, you can do it." She kneeled down beside him, setting aside her crutches. She rubbed his face. "You can make it." She looked over at Paige. "Can I give him some more water?"

"Sure."

Now that Abby had seen it done, she imitated Paige's actions. She filled the syringe and lifted his little head to give him a drink.

Paige watched. "I think I will go and get more warm water. The vet will be here in a little while. Keep rubbing him, ok?"

"I will," Abby replied.

Paige let her take another syringe of water before she headed back to the house.

When she returned, she looked at the two muddy specimens in the stall. Abby was seated with the foal's head in her lap. She was covered in mud from head to foot; her auburn hair was matted with dried mud. She looked like she had gotten into a mud fight or taken a mud bath with the colt.

"How did you get him out?" Paige asked.

Abby looked at her for a moment, then began to explain how the cougar slapped the colt. That made the baby roll up, which got its front feet loose. He was able to get them on more solid ground, but his hind end was still stuck. "So when the cat was ready to pounce, I panicked and started screaming and waving my arms. I took off my sweatshirt and waved it around like a mad woman."

Paige grinned.

"When I thought the cat was gone, I got over next to him and got my shirt around his neck. I pulled and he just kind of popped out. But as he stood up, I slipped and fell just where he had been. I heard a hiss and a growl. I couldn't get my balance, then I heard Blue barking. She took off after that cat like a shot."

Abby looked at Blue sitting outside the stall. "She is amazing. I never have seen anything like that. She really wanted to save this baby. Do you think that is why she wanted to go to the spring this morning?"

"Very well could be, Abbs. She might have wanted to protect you too." Paige looked down at her dog. She was the one animal that never asked anything of anybody and was always there. All she ever wanted was to be part of the family.

"Blue, you are a pretty special girl," Abigail said, thinking for the first time that she might have been in danger too. Blue wiggled her tail.

Abby took another syringe full of water, lifted the baby's head, and again squirted it in his mouth. He wasn't shaking anymore.

Paige went and got a soft brush and started to brush the baby curls and his shaggy coat.

"We got you, Cougar. You are going to be fine."

Paige was concerned, "Abby, you know this is not our colt right?"

Abby looked at her stunned. "I found him!" she said defiantly. "I saved him. He should be mine."

"It doesn't work that way, Abby. He has a mom out there somewhere and we need to find her. As soon as we get him stable, I am going to have to make a few phone calls and see if we can find his mother and his owner."

Abby was quiet for a moment. She touched his soft baby nose. His little whiskers curled around his mouth and nose. She knew if he did make it, he should be with his mom. But if no one claimed him, she was going to put up a fight to keep him.

"Alright," she sighed.

"Alright then, let's get his legs moving so he gets his circulation going again. We need to get him up. Go and get me a halter out of the tack room," Paige directed.

Abby looked at her questioningly. She had never been in the tack room except to get the syringe out of the top drawer. Not knowing what a halter was or what it looked like had her feeling lost.

Paige realized her error. After sending Abigail to get a blanket and her getting one from the house instead of all the horse blankets that were right there in the tack room, Paige should have had an idea of how lost this girl was on saving the colt. Well, she might not know where things were or what they were called, but she sure had the gumption to do what she set her mind to.

"Here, let me show you." Paige got up, walked to the tack room, and opened the door.

Abby noticed the three saddles along the side wall, the big horse blanket hanging on the back wall, and bridles hanging over a work bench that had a small refrigerator at the corner of it. She looked at the drawer where she had gotten the syringe. It seemed like everything had its place.

Page interrupted Abby's thoughts. "Whatever you need will be in this room when it comes to horses."

They heard a pickup pull up as they grabbed the smallest halter they could find.

"Hey, Tom," Paige said as she stepped out of the tack room.

"Hey, Paige, what do we have here?" Tom asked as his tall, lean frame stepped into the shadow of the barn.

"Don't know exactly, but the little guy sure needs a little help," Paige stated as she guided him to the stall.

Tom walked into the corral-style stall and saw the little guy lying on the sawdust. The only things that moved on him were his sides. The rest was dead still. The colt didn't even twitch an ear or blink an eye as Tom walked up to him. "Hey, little man," he said as he bent down and opened up one eyelid. An almost dead stare looked back at him. The baby's eye dilated a little, then Tom lifted the upper lip and checked his gums and tongue. They looked almost white instead of the pink normally found on a healthy horse.

Tom checked the colt for some kind of injury, running his experienced hands down his neck, his legs, his little back, his shoulders, his hips, then took his temperature. The baby just laid there. "There are no scratch marks on him except on his hip and a couple of scrapes on his legs. Other than that," Tom evaluated, "I don't find anything physically wrong with him." He grabbed his stethoscope and was quiet again. He listened to the colt's heart, his breathing, and his gut for any movement. "His heart rate and temperature are both dangerously low," Tom said as he took the stethoscope out of his ears. He had witnessed this before on older horses that had dealt with trauma and exhaustion, most didn't pull out of it. The baby just lay there, not caring what anyone was doing to him. He had given up on life. Tom looked over at Paige to be direct and honest as he slightly shook his head. "His temp is pretty low and his gut has shut down. I don't know what happened to him, but…" He paused as he saw a muddy tear-streaked girl standing next to Paige for the first time.

He took a breath. He had to regroup his thoughts and his directness on this one. He had been working since four that morning and his eyes were tired, his mind a little muddled, letting his experience take over where his compassion seemed to be a little weak this afternoon. He knew he should have exchanged pleasantries and assessed the situation a little better, but he also knew he had another horse that needed his immediate attention and was stuck in a cattle guard. He took a breath and put that to the side for now, facing the muddy colt and tear-streaked face of a muddy girl.

"If we can get him to realize the monster is gone, his body might come back full force, but right now, Paige, he doesn't think there is any reason to live."

Abby looked at him. "But he wanted to live. He was fighting for his life when the cougar was there."

Tom looked at Paige. "I will give him some electrolytes with some vitamins in an IV that might help with the trauma. I don't know if he will pull out of it or not, but…" Tom paused, looking at Abigail. "If he faced off with a cougar and lived to tell about it, he might just be a little scrapper."

Abby squatted down next to Cougar and gave him a pep talk with tears running down her dirty face. "You gotta live, Cougar. It is not so bad. Please, Cougar, don't give up." Her heart ached for him to understand.

Tom walked out to get an IV from his truck and Paige followed. "Tom, have you heard of anyone losing their colt?" Paige asked quietly.

"No, but I would sure call around and see what you can find. Jim Curry has a couple of broodmares. He is a ways off from here, Paige. I can't imagine that little guy getting this far."

"Yeah, I thought I would call Jim first," Paige replied as they headed back into the barn.

Tom squatted down and felt around on the baby's neck. He put the needle under the skin and searched for the little dehydrated artery that would help this guy live. With experienced hands, he found it first try. He attached the IV hose then taped all the way around his neck and attached the IV. He turned it up for a fast drip and waited.

"It looks like both of you got to roll in the mud today," Tom said with a grin, hoping to ease a little stress.

"Actually, Abby was the one who went head to head with that cat."

"Yeah, but Blue is the one that chased it off." Abby looked over at the dog lying quietly next to the stall door.

"Really?" Tom said. "So what happened?"

Abigail once again began her story of going to the spring. Tom and Paige listened.

"I have seen some pretty strange things happen," Tom said as he looked down at the baby. "Let's see if we can get this little guy to stand up." Tom rocked him back and forth, and the colt leaned up. Then with a little help from Paige and Abby, they lifted him to his feet with the IV still in his neck. His little legs were weak and shaky at first, but they soon found that they could hold his weight and he stood spraddled. They stabilized him standing, then Abby grabbed the brush and started brushing his muddy golden coat. His eyes were still only half open.

"I am going to go ahead and give him one more bag of fluids. I think that might just be what he needs," Tom said as he stood watching him for a few minutes and checked his heart rate again. "You know, Paige, I think I would watch him for a couple of days and get his mom here as soon as you can find her. But I don't think I would send him home. If he isn't any better in the next six to eight hours, give me a holler. You should notice a change in him. If you girls can make him move around, that would be the best idea. Don't let him sleep too long. We want to keep his kidneys working. Do you have any Banamine, Paige?"

"Yes."

"I gave him one shot that should last for a while, but we just don't know what he is going to do. Are you comfortable with pulling the IV, Paige?" Tom asked as he looked at the colt again.

"Yes, I can do that."

"Alright then, I have a horse that got caught in a cattle guard, so I am going to have to leave you girls. Abby, you keep a good eye on him and keep him moving around a little at a time alright. That is a great idea brushing him, it helps with the circulation."

Abby looked over at Tom. It made her feel good to be wanted and needed and looked at like a helper, not a cripple. With that assignment she boldly said, "Alright, I will."

Paige shook Tom's hand. "Thanks again for coming out. Sure do appreciate it."

"No problem, Paige. Call me if you don't see any difference in him in a couple hours, alright?"

"Alright."

Tom got in his truck and started the engine. He looked at the barn once more before driving off.

The baby stood with his head relaxed, but at least he looked like he wasn't going to die. Paige put the halter on him. "Here, see if you can lead him around." She handed the lead to Abby.

"What if he falls down?" Abby asked as she tried to tug on the lead.

"Well I guess we will pick him up."

"He just looks so tired."

"He is, but he has to keep moving," Paige said. "Go ahead and walk him around the stall, Abby, just a little. We want him to feel like he is alright."

Abby took the lead line in one hand with the oversized halter hanging on Cougar's little head and started to pull him. With her other hand, she hung onto her crutch.

"Go easy with him. I will be back in a few minutes." Paige went to go make some phone calls to see if anyone would claim the little guy.

***

The phone rang twice when Jim Curry, a soft-spoken man, answered. "Hello?"

"Hey, Jim, this is Paige. How are you?"

"Doing pretty good, Paige. Kind of in a dilemma right now but hoping things will work out."

"What do you have going on?" Paige asked concerned. "You aren't missing a palomino colt by chance?"

"Actually I am. He has been missing since this morning. There are cougar tracks but can't make heads nor tails of them, Paige. I have the mare here and she is missing her baby something terrible."

Paige was quiet as Jim Curry continued his story of the missing colt.

"I can't find any blood, and I don't see any drag marks. But I am sure a cougar had something to do with it. I have lost his trail and can't seem to pick it up again. I have been looking all morning." The urgency in his voice was clearly audible. He was quiet then it dawned on him, "Did you find my colt?"

"Well, Jim, I think he is yours. He is a palomino about two or three weeks old. Abby found him bogged down in our spring earlier today. She had to fight off a cougar to save him. I don't know how he got clear over here, but I figured I would give you a call first. I knew you have a couple of broodmares."

"This little guy is a stud colt and pretty powerfully built," Jim said. "He is out of your dad's stud horse, actually, Paige. I sure would hate to lose the little guy."

"Well," Paige said, "we have him down in our barn. Just had Tom take a look at him and we think he is going to be alright. Can you milk that mare out and bring her down here? Tom doesn't want to move him for a day or so, and I am sure he would like to get a bite to eat."

"How in the hell did he get clear over to your place?"

"I don't know, Jim, but we will tell you what we know as soon as you get here." Paige paused. "You are more than welcome to leave him here for a day or so until he gets back on his feet. Right now he is still pretty weak. Come and take a look, Jim, and tell me what you want to do."

"I think if he is pretty weak, I can just bring the mare over and let her be with him. We can put a panel up between them until he gets to feeling better. You're probably right, Paige, I will milk her out here, then take her over. She is going to be pretty excited to see him.

"See you in a bit then, Jim."

"Yep, Paige, see you in a bit."

Paige hung up the phone, sitting for a moment, thinking of all that had just happened. She looked out the window and saw Abby working at leading the colt just inside the sunlight of the barn door. The struggle of working her legs, the crutches, and helping a little colt learn to want to live again. *Life is ironic,* she thought as she watched through the window. *How did these two souls find each other?*

Not an hour later, Jim pulled up with stock trailer in tow. He pulled down by the barn and got out of the truck with a soda bottle half full of milk in his hand.

Paige walked out to meet him. He had a grin on his face. "She wasn't happy, but we got it done." He handed Paige the bottle with a triumphant look on his face as he tipped back his hat.

They strode into the barn. Abby was cradling the baby's head, brushing his neck, and he was sound asleep.

"Here, Abbs, let's give him something he would like to have." She emptied the little bucket of water and poured in the mare's milk. Abby filled the syringe and put it to his cheek like she had done with the water.

The colt just swallowed. Abby gave him another syringe full, then a third. Still the colt didn't change his expression.

"His gut had started shutting down because of the trauma, according to Tom, so we want to take this a little at a time. Here in a few more minutes we will get him up again and let him see his mom."

The mare nickered in the trailer. The wind must have shifted, and she knew her baby was close. The baby twitched his ears.

"Yep, he is going to be fine," Jim said. "Just fine."

While Abby got him up and led him around his little stall again, Paige and Jim grabbed a panel and tied it in the center of the stall. That way the mare could see her baby and maybe nuzzle him a little but would not step on him in her nervousness.

Jim went out to the trailer and unloaded the mare.

Without hesitation the mare followed the big man into the barn and to the stall. The mare started talking to her baby.

Paige spoke to Abby. "Bring the baby to the door and let the mare have a look at him. Just keep that IV line away from the mare. Better yet, that IV looks done. Let's just pull it before we bring her in here." She walked to the tack room and grabbed tape and gauze. In a few swift actions, the IV was out, the gauze was in place, and the tape was around his neck.

Abby watched surprised at how Paige was so sure of what to do. Her hands moved smoothly and effortlessly as she brought the bandage around the baby's neck, held it, then took a pair of schoolroom scissors and snipped it off the roll.

Paige looked at her work, making sure that he was not bleeding, then patted Abby on the shoulder. "There you go. Now you can take him out to the mare."

Cougar seemed happy to see his mom as Jim led the mare to him, she nuzzled and talked and cleaned her baby. Milk was running down her legs.

Jim grinned. "Yep. A couple of days and we should be good."

He looked over at Abby. "So you are the one who found him, huh?"

Abby looked up at the big man. Nervously, she answered, "Yes."

"Well I can't tell you how much I appreciate that. I was thinking we had lost him for good." He walked over and put a hand on her shoulder.

"I will show you where he was when I found him if you would like to see. I was going to take Paige down there anyway."

"Sure," Jim answered. "Whenever you guys are ready."

Page looked at the panel, checking the sturdiness, and threw a little hay in for the mare, satisfied that she had plenty of room to move around and her baby was comfortable. "We could go now if you want."

Abby leaned on her crutches and headed to the spring, Paige and Jim close behind.

Abby felt comfortable talking as they walked. She focused on her walking as she traveled down the path. When she got down to where she had heard the noise, she got nervous about the incident. She peeked around the corner like she had done when the baby was mired in the mud.

She looked at the area and then back at Jim and Paige and kind of felt silly. Although she felt better having them there and Blue at her heels, she still glanced at the tree where the cougar had taken refuge. Blue took the lead and started smelling the ground where the cougar had been. She was excited but not threatened like before, so Abby continued on her trek to the mud hole that she and the baby had created. There—still in the mud where she had left it—was her sweatshirt. Jim reached down, grabbed a stick, and snagged the shirt.

"Boy, looks like you had quite a challenge on your hands. You got him out of here?" he said, as he pulled the shirt out of the bog.

"Yeah, with the help of Blue I did." Abby reached over and stroked the dog's head as she stood at her side. Abby finished telling her story of the sweatshirt and how Blue ran past her when she fell in the mud.

Jim took the muddy shirt off the stick and shook it a little to see if any mud would come off. None did. "Well, all I can say is you are one brave girl," he said in admiration. "Which way did the cougar go?"

"Blue ran that way." She pointed toward the right through the tall grass and into the timber close to the fence line.

"It went right back onto my place, Paige. So there has got to be a den or something around. We will have to keep an eye out and maybe bring some hounds to run," Jim stated with worry. "I leave them alone if they leave me alone."

"I know a guy on the other side of town who has a couple of hounds. I will see if he wants to run them and cause a little pressure on this cat," Paige said quietly. "Seems that cat is getting pretty cozy running around here."

They talked for a while as they watched the water run from the spring. Then they headed back to the barn. "I am thinking it must have been a young cat that chased and teased him all the way over here," Jim said thinking out loud.

"Or it could have been a female teaching her cubs to hunt. Especially if you had tracks all over your place, Jim," Paige answered. "Tom had an emergency of a horse in a cattle guard too, seems like something is happening around here to stir up the horses."

"Guess we will find out soon enough," Jim said as he looked back the way Abby had pointed. "They're getting pretty close to home. Be careful out here, Paige. My neighbor on the other side of me had a cougar in the rafters of her barn not more than four weeks ago."

"We will keep our eyes open, Jim. Now that we know Blue is aware of them, we will be listening to her a little more," Paige answered.

The conversation drifted and hovered over horses and cougars all the way back to the barn.

As they entered to check on the mare one more time, Jim said, "Seems like there has been quite a bit of livestock accidents around this area, maybe the Fish and Game would have an idea what is going on."

"Well, it is worth a try," Paige said as she checked the water in the stall. The mare was eating quietly with her head close to her baby. Cougar was sleeping soundly. Hearing his mother eating seemed to settle him. His breathing was slower and less stressed.

"I think we have everything under control here, Jim," Paige said as they started walking toward Jim's rig.

Jim got into his truck and pushed in the clutch. "Well girls, I sure appreciate you taking care of my horses. If you need anything call me, alright? I guess I will see you in a couple of days."

"We will," Paige said as he turned on his key. His pickup engine came to life with a soft purr. He put it in gear and pulled out. They both waved at him as he left.

6

Craig stepped off the last plane in the Boise Airport. It had been a long day—three two-hour layovers. He had finally made it to Idaho and could have kissed the ground. Thank God he traveled alone. He had his carry-on slung over his shoulder as he walked out into the waiting area.

Jim Curry waited nervously in the crowded airport, noticing all the different types of people coming and going to unknown places. He twirled his son's cowboy hat in his hands. He had subconsciously grabbed it as he walked out the door of the house. He felt kind of silly holding it as he had his own on his head, but it seemed to be a link or connection to the boy he once had. As people filtered out of the terminal, Jim's eyes searched for a familiar face, stance or voice as the traffic jam of people greeted each other and walked into the lobby area. Still no Craig, he began to fidget as he thought he might be at the wrong place. He looked at his paper again. *Nope this is it*, he thought as he tried to gain confidence. Then, almost the last one out, Jim recognized his son right away. With his long cowboy stride and straight shoulders, he knew it was him. He was thicker than Jim remembered him, more square and prominent in his stature.

Craig had an aged look to him for his young life, almost like Jim's dad did when he came back from the Korean War—a look of a deep knowledge of life's trials. It was something that Jim himself could not explain nor had he experienced. But he'd seen a deep sorrow beyond everyday life in the heart of this young man.

As Jim watched his only son walk toward him, he had a flashback of Craig's first steps, riding his first horse, roping his first calf, coming out of the bucking chute on his first saddle bronc at the high school rodeo. Now here he stood, almost a stranger. Yet there was a connection so strong it could be no other than his own blood.

Craig saw his father's cowboy hat across the way and headed straight for him. He walked up to him and held out his hand. Jim took it and grabbed his son into an embrace. Craig almost melted in his dad's arms. For a moment in time, he felt the strength, power, and safety of his father as if he were a child once more. All the hustle and hurry around the two men melted away, and a sense of completeness filled the moment. Craig closed his eyes as a tear ran down his cheek.

"It is good to see you, my son." Jim released him and brushed his hand across his face, trying to dry the moisture that had run down his cheek while getting a better look at his son. "I think this belongs to you." Jim handed Craig his cowboy hat.

Craig smiled and took it from his dad, slipping it on his head. "Fits like a glove," he said as he creased the front of the hat out of habit.

"You have filled out a little since I last saw you," Jim said as he slapped his son's shoulder a couple of times and grinned.

"I have been working out a little, Dad…been doing things to keep me busy," he said as he looked to the ground as if embarrassed by the comment while wiping his cheek dry.

They walked over to get the rest of Craig's luggage, which ended up only being a duffle bag, then headed for the parking lot toward the truck.

It felt good to be out in the open air so close to home. Even the smell of Boise couldn't take away the scent of sagebrush and high-desert air that awaited him. Craig took a deep breath and let it out slowly. "So tell me, Dad, what has been going on with you? Has anything been exciting since I have been gone?" He looked at his dad, who looked older than he had the last time Craig had seen him. But he still had the stance of a big man. Craig had to smile. He always thought his dad looked like John Wayne, and today was no different—a big man with a little age in his eyes and the strength of ten men. A feeling of peace filled his heart.

"Oh not a whole lot, Craig. But this last week we had a little cougar incident that got me stirred up. I have a couple of broodmares and bred one of them to Abe Cason's stud horse, Shorty. Well the colt went missing the other day, looks like he got chased clear over to Paige Cason's place. Abby found him mired in the mud at Paige's spring. Guess a cougar was teasing him."

"Who is Abby?" Craig asked casually. Just the name Paige Cason made his heart rate pick up.

"Oh, she is a girl staying with Paige," Jim said ignoring the inquiry and focusing on the colt. Abby calls him Cougar, and I think it is going to stick. Anyway," Jim continued, "I am going to go down tomorrow and get him and the mare. They have been in her barn for about five days. Abby is pretty happy to play with the colt." Jim smiled.

"Does Paige have a kid?" Craig asked, kind of curious. He hadn't thought of her for some time. He could remember when he was a kid and being at the fair grounds at the horse show. He remembered how she rode into the arena to stop Piper, who was a stampeding horse dragging one of Craig's friends, Samantha Greenly. He also remembered going out to her house and spending the entire day talking and helping Abe Cason build corrals. And thinking of Patricia's cooking, his mouth started to water. There was nothing like her home cooked meal. It all seemed like a lifetime ago. Then coming back to Oregon and helping the Cason's get settled in their new place, celebrating Paige's birthday, and helping Abe with a couple of colts. Craig's mind was overflowing with memories and good times.

"God, Dad, it is good to be home," Craig said with a sigh. "It just feels right." As they got to the pickup, Craig lifted his duffle bag from his shoulder and tossed it in the back like it was his saddle rigging from his rodeo days.

"It is good to have you home, kid," his dad replied. "Real good to have you home. And to answer your question, no Paige does not have a kid. She is fostering Abby for a while as they try to find a more suitable home for her."

"What is she like a puppy or something? A more suitable home... What happened?"

Jim started explaining about Abby and how she ended up at Paige's doorstep. Then he left it there. "You know, I think if you are that curious, you ought to go over and ask Paige," he said with a smile. "I know just enough to be dangerous. I will send you over to pick up that mare and colt tomorrow."

"Sounds good, Dad. Would be happy to," Craig said with a grin.

Jim pulled the pickup out onto I-84 heading west. He had all he needed from Idaho. It was time to go home.

7

Paige looked at the blank paper in front of her. What was she going to put on it? How was it going to look? She paused a moment to envision her idea. Her mind raced with all that she needed to do. She really needed to go to bed, but there was the checkbook that she needed to balance too. She promised her mom that she would have this designing project done in the next couple of days. Designing barns and ranch layouts had been Paige's job for the last couple of years, and she felt good about the work she had done. But now it seemed like there was not enough time in the day. So she resigned herself to draw in early mornings or the evening when she had quiet, solace, and a place where she could think. Paige sighed and began with a stroke of her pencil. The angle seemed wrong, so she tried again. Her eyes were tired and her fingers felt heavy, but she tried again to make a mark that was a starting point. *Don't draw the whole thing*, she thought. *Set a goal of one thing—the walls, get the angle. Let the pencil do the talking.* She closed her eyes again and just began to envision what she wanted. She let the pencil do the rest.

She lost herself one more time in the strokes of creating. The one place where everything could make sense to her and she could create what she wanted, exactly how she saw things. The place where she could melt away and have no worries of the outside world.

She looked at the clock as she put the finishing touches on the barn. It was eleven thirty. The house was completely quiet. Blue was lying at her feet sound asleep. The quiet was almost deafening as she closed her eyes and stretched. This seemed to be the only time she could slow down enough to draw. She thought back to when she was a girl and all the drawing she had done. Most she had saved tucked away in a box in the closet. She hadn't looked at them for years now. Where had the time gone? She smiled as she thought of the first person to ever see some of her drawings. How her heart had thumped in her throat as she opened up the notebook and tried to find something worth showing him. Craig Curry, a tall lanky kid back then. She remembered that day as if it were yesterday. She smiled at the memory of how easy he was to talk to, how they laughed, and how he loved her work. He took her sketchbook away from her so that he could see what she had done. How he had slowly turned each page and looked at the detail and definition of her work. She remembered how her heart skipped a beat as she listened to him. And before he left, he told her he was moving and then gave her a kiss.

Paige closed her eyes again. *I wonder what he is doing now? That is too funny*, she thought, *I haven't thought about Craig in a long time.* The thought of his kiss made her feel warm inside. *Huh...* she thought for a moment of the few dates she had been on. None of them was as sweet or as memorable or as simple as her first kiss.

She closed her sketchbook and laid her hands on the cover as a warm sensation went through her body. She opened it back up and turned the pages, passing by the barns and the yards, the layouts, measurements, and design sketches to a fresh piece of paper. She looked at it a moment and within seconds her pencil started sketching the outline of a horse's face—something she had not done in years. She was drawing from the heart.

It flowed out of her like water from a tap as she continued to put pencil to paper, and the image began to appear before her eyes. She had no thought or concept of what she was doing, just the feel of pencil stroking across the paper, the motion and the belief that it needed to be drawn.

When she had finished, she laid down her pencils and looked at her work. It was a single arched neck of a horse, a hazel-eyed buckskin with a war bridle on. A single feather was attached to the tether right behind his ear that was cocked back toward the rider, who didn't exist in the piece. He held no expression of worry or fear, but he had a look of spirit, life, and understanding. Underneath the picture, she wrote *From the Heart*.

Paige sat there and looked at her work, pleased with the outcome yet curious where it had come from. She closed her sketchbook again, heard the soft hum of the refrigerator turn on, and looked at the clock. It was two fifteen in the morning. It was time to go to bed. She set her sketchbook down and turned out the light. Blue followed her to her room, happy to finally go to bed.

8

As the sun began to rise, Abby brought her hand up to cover her eyes from the light that peeked in between the curtains. She wanted to sleep a few more hours, but for some reason sleep was eluding her. She rolled over, pulled the pillow over her head, and covered her face.

Well that isn't going to work, she thought, *I can't breathe like that*. So she rolled back over, dropped her hands down to her sides and sighed. She did notice that her leg was getting stronger the more she walked. She was able to balance on it now without feeling like it was going to collapse. She brought her left leg up to her chest and did a press with it, then straightened it out again. She lifted it again, wrapped her arms around it, and squeezed again. Then she did the right. If she kept doing her exercises, maybe she wouldn't be crippled.

She thought of her mud bath a few nights before to get the goo off her after falling in the spring. It didn't come off as easily as it went on. She smiled. She had ended up pulling the plug, draining the tub, and taking a shower to get the caked mud off her. Then it took her twenty minutes to clean the tub.

Her mother would have been worried sick about her getting dirty and having the tub so dirty. She thought of how her mom would fuss with her hair and make sure everything was perfect.

Abby could hear her mom's voice, "Be careful going down the stairs, honey." Or, "Don't cut yourself with those scissors." "Here let me cut that up for you." Abby felt that she was smothered most of the time, but she missed her mother's protective nature and her father's laugh. Here with Paige, it was different. Paige didn't make her do anything. It was more of a suggestion.

Somehow her life seemed to have shifted and she was trying to make sense of it. Trying to adjust to the new but hold on to the memories of what was. How does a person hold on and let go at the same time? Would she forget who she was or was she scared of who she might be?

Blue came into the bedroom to say good morning. She laid her head on the bed and stood patiently to be petted. Abby brought her hand out and rubbed Blue's head for a moment. Then she leaned up and said, "Well, ole girl, guess it is time to get up."

She swung her legs over the bed and reached for her crutches. *I have got to check on that baby,* she thought as she slipped on her jeans and tied her shoes.

Paige had gotten a couple of hours of sleep and was at the kitchen table. She had her colored pencils and sketchpad and was coloring the barn that she had created the night before.

Abby looked at what Paige had done. She sat at the table and cupped her chin in the palms of her hands propped up by her elbows, sleep still lurking in her eyes. "What are you doing?"

"I need to get these plans done for a client of ours. Just have to put on a couple of finishing touches before I give them to Mom," Paige replied.

"Oh."

"What is going on with you? You're not usually up this early in the morning."

"I don't know. I wanted to go check on Cougar," Abby answered and then she sighed. "I just can't sleep."

"Why not?" Paige asked, picking up her pencils and folding the tablet closed.

"I don't know," Abby paused, "maybe because I miss my parents. Or maybe because I am mad at them or maybe because I feel like I am the blame for them dying. I just don't know for sure." Abby was surprised at her honesty with Paige, but she continued. "Maybe I am afraid that I will forget them. Seems like my mind is all messed up with all these questions and feelings. Sometimes I have a hard time shutting it off. The more I don't want to think about them, the more it seems they come into my mind."

"I just got in from checking Cougar," Paige said. "And he is doing just fine." She grabbed her coffee walked over to fill her cup. "Well is there anything that I might be able to help you out with?"

Abby looked at Paige for a moment as if contemplating what to say, then just blurted out her question. "Why do bad things happen to people?"

"Well that is a pretty loaded question, Abby," Paige answered. She thought for a moment. "I could give you a thousand reasons for bad things happening, but there should be a better question to ask yourself."

"Like what?"

"Why not ask a question like how amazing is life?"

"But, that doesn't answer my question, though."

Paige thought for a moment then said, "When things happen to me and I don't like it, I have two choices." She paused. "I can either feel sorry for myself and ask, 'Why me?' Or I can ask myself, 'What can I learn from this?' Then I evaluate it from there." Paige paused a minute to let Abby think about it. Then she continued.

"If you were to ask yourself, 'Why did my parents die?' you could think up so many reasons why they did. But how many answers would be true? Or how many would you claim to be true?" Paige waited. "Because in all honesty, Abby, you will never be able to answer that question."

Paige paused again to think of how to simplify. "So I guess what I am getting at, Abby, is instead of asking questions that you can't honestly answer, ask questions that can help guide you."

"Like, what did my parents teach me?" Abby asked hesitantly.

"Yes, something like that. What are my strengths they have given me?" Paige again stopped and waited for Abby to respond. She saw a tear run down Abby's cheek.

"I didn't get a chance to say goodbye." Abby started to sob as the words escaped her lips. "I was so mad at them for making me go with them. I thought it was the end of the world sitting in the back seat of that car. How could I have been so stupid?" The words were finally escaping her as she spoke the worst thoughts that had been plaguing her heart. "I can't seem to get them out of my mind." She sobbed, "I miss them so much it hurts. There is an emptiness in my heart that I am afraid won't fill. I am afraid I will forget them." She didn't care that anyone saw her cry. She just didn't care anymore. She felt Paige's arms encircle her, felt her body go limp and sobs escape from her heart.

Paige felt tears run down her face. She pulled Abigail to her and let her cry. There were no words for comfort, no promises, just listening. Listening to a girl with a broken heart who was uncertain of her future and who she was.

Paige handed her a tissue as Abby began to quiet herself down.

"I don't think one tissue is going to work," Abby stated as she wiped her eyes and started to blow her nose. "I think you better just give me the box." She gave a half-hearted laugh.

Paige grabbed the box from the counter and took a couple for herself first before handing it over to Abby. "I don't know what it feels like to lose both of your parents. I can't even imagine what you have gone through. But I do want you to know that you are a very special young lady and you are smart and brave. It is not your fault they died. I don't think you will ever forget your parents, but I think it is important to honor them by continuing to live."

"What do you mean? I am living," Abby questioned her.

"Yes you are, but how are you living? Right now you don't have a choice on where you live, but you do have a choice on how you live." Paige thought for a moment, then continued. "Just like being in this house or being outside. One day you decided to get out of the house and be a part of life. And thank God you did, you found Jim Curry's colt and was able to use your smarts to get him out. You chose that Abby. Does that make sense?"

"Well, yeah, I suppose. But what does that have to do with missing my parents?"

"I am thinking that if you wanted to honor your parents, you would choose to do things that make you happy and help you grow through life. That is what they would have wanted, I think. And even if it wasn't, why not mix it up a little bit—rebel and do it anyway." Paige winked at Abby and Abby grinned.

"You are a smart girl. You've got a good head on your shoulders. All I am saying is use it." Paige took a sip of coffee. "I have to go get hay today. Do you want to go with me?"

"What can I do?" Abby answered.

"Now see, that is what I am talking about." Paige smiled. "Good question. Shall we find out?"

Abby looked at her for a moment then smiled. "Yes, let's do."

"Let's go turn the horses out and get things cleaned up here. I want to get the hay before the heat of the day," Paige requested.

"Do you want Curry's mare and Cougar out in the front paddock?" Abby asked, excited to play with the colt.

"Sure, do you want to do that for me?"

"Yes, I think I can."

Alright then, I will turn Libby and the other mares out in the back pasture. I'll get the stalls cleaned out, and we will be ready to roll."

Abby crutched her way to the barn, taking a deep breath of morning air. For the first time in a long time, she felt like she could breathe again. She thought back to where she was a year ago, calling her friends, going to malls, and thinking all that was important. But now here she was working with horses, having a thousand-pound animal following her around because of a rope around its neck. She heard them nicker softly at her as she approached the barn, smelling the hay, the sunlight on her face.

She entered the barn where Cougar and the mare stood waiting. "Let's get you out of here," Abby said as she looked at the contraption called a halter. Paige had always haltered the horses, but not today. She looked at the rope with holes all over it. She took it off the peg and analyzed it. "Ok, now I watched Paige do this the other day and she made it look so simple." She turned it around to try to figure out front and back. But the more she looked at it, the more complicated it got.

She turned it over again, then she turned it upside down. "This just can't be this hard to do," she said to herself as she walked to the mare. As she got up to her, the mare dropped her head to have the halter put on. "Ok, so this goes here and that has to go over your nose and this strap goes over there." Abby tied the knot and looked at her work. "That is not it. I don't think you are supposed to have a line down your face, and where does that hole go?" She grabbed at the horse's cheek where there was another hole. "That doesn't look right at all." She sighed, then undid the knot and tried it again.

Now there was a hole on the other side and the strap that needed to be tied was under the mare's jaw as she lifted the two holes over the ears. "This doesn't look right." Abby sighed. The mare was getting anxious and was ready to get out and move around. Abby pulled on the halter and the mare moved. The halter stayed on the mare, so she opened the gate and the mare and Cougar came out. Cougar was ready to play. It was hard to believe five days ago he was close to death and today he was wanting to buck and play.

Abby felt tense as she watched the baby run past her. "Cougar," she said a little nervous, "be careful." She was trying to handle her crutches and the mare at the same time. The mare ignored the colt. The halter hung precariously on the horse's head, but she respected it being there and waited for the girl to walk her to the paddock. Cougar came dashing back and circled around them. He came up from behind and cut her off. There was six feet to go to get to the paddock. Abby was feeling anxious to get this guy in the paddock.

Paige stopped what she was doing and watched. The halter Abby had put on the mare was on backward, so the line that went under the jaw was in the middle of her face and the two cheek holes were over her ears. The piece that was supposed to be tied just behind the ears was down by her lower jaw. She had to grin to herself but said nothing.

Cougar kept bucking around, but the aged mare was familiar with all the commotion and was just happy to get outside and get some grass. Abby stopped and reset her crutches. Cougar came around the back side of her and brushed against her knocking her into the mare. The mare sidestepped and made Abby lose her balance, falling farther toward the mare. The mare froze as the crutch hit her side and Abby grasped for something to break her fall, grabbing hold of the mare's long black mane. The mare waited for Abby's fate, but Abby regained her balance, picked the crutch up from the mare's shoulder and stoked the mare's neck. Cougar was still bucking and playing, not a care in the world.

Abby gritted her teeth and summoned up the courage to finish what she had started. "Boy you have your hands full with this guy," she said to the mare. She got to the gate with a sigh. She opened it and led the mare in. Cougar didn't want to go in because he was bucking and playing outside. He stopped to eat a little grass and smell a couple of unfamiliar objects. "Come on, Cougar," Abby called. "Come on." She called him like a dog, but he was having none of it. He had a whole world to explore and he was ready to take it on.

Paige decided to help. "Lead her out and then take her back in all the way to the middle of the paddock if you need to. Make him feel like he is missing something."

Abby did as she was instructed. She led the mare with her upside down halter back out of the paddock. With her crutches, she hobbled back into the paddock and kept walking. Cougar found the gate, came bounding in and raced in front of the mare. Abby looked back at the gate and knew that if she led the mare back toward the gate, Cougar would want to run through it. So seeing the distance she had to go, she untied the halter and turned the mare loose. The mare dropped her head to eat while Cougar bounced around her. Abby quickly crutched her way back to the gate and closed it. She leaned up against the fence and sighed.

"You alright?" Paige asked as she walked up with a forkful of hay and threw it over the fence.

"Yeah," Abby replied. "I didn't think it would be that hard to get that cute little baby in a corral."

"They are pretty unpredictable. And that little guy right there, he is built for speed."

Paige leaned against the fence and watched him. If this was out of her dad's stud, Shorty, he could sure throw some really nice babies. She began to wonder about Libby. She was ten this year. She might be a pretty good broodmare. She thought back to when she sold Libby to John Greenly and how he was going to make a broodmare out of her. That didn't work out so well. Libby didn't seem like she wanted to be a broodmare. She wanted to be Paige's horse. Her heart filled with pride as she thought of those summer days, driving up into the Greenly's Driveway and having Libby race the truck all the way to the barn.

Paige yearned to step onto Libby today and go for a ride.

Abby watched him skirt around the corral, "I think he needs a playmate."

He nibbled on some grass for a few minutes then took off at a full run across the paddock. He circled around, ran right straight for his mom, and then slammed on his brakes stopping just before impact. Then he dodged right, left, right then left again as if asking, "Which way do I go? Which way do I go?" Then he took off like a bullet the other direction and circled around again.

"Boy he looks like he is crazy," Abby said as she watched him bounce around.

Paige finally responded to Abby's comments. "He is bred to be a cutting horse. Those are his natural moves."

"A cutting horse? What is that?" Abby was envisioning a horse with an apron on, cutting things with a knife. "That doesn't even make sense."

"When people go out to gather cattle," Paige stated, "they choose what cow they want, and *cut* that cow out of the herd. Say you had a sick baby calf and you need to get it to the barn, you would want the mom to go with it. So you would sort her and her baby away from the herd to get her to the barn. You would cut her out. It is the horse's job to make sure the cow stays out of the herd and goes where they need to take it. It looks like an amazing dance, and a horse should be able to balance itself and be catty on its feet."

Paige watched him. Then said, "This yellow horse here is bred to do that, and right now he is just learning how to dance."

They watched in silence for a while until Cougar had run himself down to being happy nibbling on grass with his mom.

"So it is almost not fair to have him in a stall, then," Abby stated as she watched him settle down.

"For me," Paige stated her opinion, "you're right. I don't like horses in stalls. These are animals that are bred to move and run. It seems that stalls are too confining. A stall has its place on a ranch, look what it did for us when that baby needed help. But to house a horse only in stalls is a little harsh I think."

Paige turned to go back to the house. She looked over and saw her mare Libby on the hillside grazing. Libby looked in Paige's direction, then dropped her head to go back to eating. Paige had a yearning to go for a ride, not a long one but one to stretch her legs and feel that magnificent horse beneath her. Maybe she might get some of her thoughts lined out. Before she could think about it any longer, she heard herself whistle for Libby. Libby picked up her head, looked at Paige again, then started heading to the barn at a trot.

"Abbs, I think I am gonna go for a ride this morning. Are you going to be alright for a while?"

Abby looked at her for a moment. "Sure."

"I will be back in a little while. Then we will get hay."

Abby watched as Libby made her way down to the barn and waited for Paige to slip the halter on. She led her to the barn and began to brush her out as Libby ate her grain quietly.

Abby wanted to go down there with Paige but thought better of it and sat on the porch with Blue. Blue laid her head on Abby's lap and waited to be petted. Abby watched as Paige slipped on Libby's bridle lifting the single rein over her head then swung on bareback. Libby's ears were up and her head was alert.

"Be back in a little while," Paige said again. Blue lifted her head as if to ask if she could go, and Paige seemed to read her mind. "No, Blue, you stay here this morning." Blue almost seemed relieved.

She nudged Libby forward. Riding felt as natural as breathing. Paige felt Libby's muscles moving underneath her, with no more effort than the power of thought from horse to the rider. She shifted her weight and turned her shoulders, and Libby instantly turned under her and started off down the road. Paige felt a lift in Libby's energy and nudged her on up into a lope, disappearing over the little rise.

***

Abby watched them go and wondered if she would ever be able to do that. She crutched her way into the house and walked around inside it. She remembered not so long ago this was the only place she wanted to be, but now it seemed suffocating. She looked at the pictures on the wall, Paige's dad, Abe, was on Shorty with a large trophy with a banner NCHA. And then there was a picture of Paige's mom, Patricia. She and Paige looked so much alike it was amazing. They almost looked like sisters. Abby wondered if Paige had any brothers or sisters. She continued looking around. She went through the bookshelf and found a photo album. She opened it up and thumbed through the pictures.

She found an old newspaper clipping with a picture of Paige and Libby. The headline read *Poor Girl saves Wealthy Man's Daughter*. She read through the article. Abby was enthralled, casting her imagination back to when Paige was a teenager. Living in a moment when Paige shined and envisioning where she had come from. Reading what she was able to do on horseback was exciting. Abby thumbed through more photos and noticed there was a senior picture of a young man with a letterman's jacket. He was good looking for the most part. She flipped the picture over and on the back. It said: *Paige, Just thinking of you. Craig.*

So that must have been her boyfriend. She thumbed through the rest of the pictures but none of them showed any more pictures of her and boys. She put the book away and started looking at the books that lined the shelves. A couple caught her eye right off and she took them off the shelf. *The Foundation of the Cutting Horse* and *The Foundation Training of Cutting Horses.* Abby started thumbing through them, looking at the pictures of all the horses and reading the names. They were funny names she would have never chosen for a horse, like Gun Smoke or Poco Lena. Really? Those two names stood out because written beside them on the border highlighted was one name word, *Shorty.* She continued to read and thumb through the pages. She closed the book and ran her hands over the cover of it. She got up, went to the fridge, pulled out some ice, and poured herself a glass of lemonade. She then headed to the porch where Blue still lay. She sat in a wicker chair, put her lemonade on the side table, and began to read. She read stories of each individual horse and how they had made their mark in the cutting world. She saw pictures of colts out of sires that looked exactly like Cougar. That was why Paige said he was bred to be a cutting horse. She sat there and read the book from beginning to end and never once touched her lemonade.

9

Craig glanced in the window. He could see someone, and they needed help. Who was it? He banged on the glass. Was it someone he knew, or was it a stranger? How would he get in there to help them? It was more like a silhouette—too dark to make the person out. He felt helpless and confused. He banged on the glass again and leaned closer, peering into the dark room to get a better look. But still he couldn't see the person clearly. He reached his hand up to shade his eyes as panic seemed to penetrate his whole body. Then he felt himself falling. Bang! He heard a thud and it startled him awake. He was lying on the floor covered in sweat.

The dreams weren't as bad as they had been in the past. He got off the floor, sat on the side of the bed, and put his foggy head in his cupped hands. He rubbed his eyes to clear his thoughts then looked at the clock. It was four thirty in the morning, so it was seven thirty back home.

He slipped on his sweat bottoms and a t-shirt, went to the kitchen, and started a pot of coffee.

He leaned on the counter for a moment as he listened to the water spit and gurgle as it started to perk. He walked over to the front door and opened it, letting the fresh air penetrate the house. Craig mindlessly glanced around the house of his youth. The white sofa he had sat on as a kid still stood in the middle of the front room with a cowhide over the back of it. The rest looked like something out of a cabin magazine—a few elk horns lying around and a Navaho rug lying in the middle of the floor with the glass coffee table on top. A brown leather recliner sat off to the side with an end table. It appeared to be where his dad liked to sit.

The place was comfortable, but it was missing a woman's touch. The coffee pot was quiet when he walked back into the kitchen. He poured a cup, headed out to the porch to clear his head, and sat to watch the morning come alive. The birds singing in the trees made him feel welcome while the horses shuffled around in the corral at the barn. He wondered what his partner John would be doing in the busy city across the country.

He read the local paper and smiled at its size. He perused through who was getting married, who made the obituary, and who had a baby, all on one page. Craig's eyes caught a glimpse of Samantha Greenly's picture. She was now Samantha Watterson, and she had just had a baby boy. "Jonathon Harley, six pounds two ounces, twenty-three inches long." *Wow!* He thought, a hotheaded girl who knew what she wanted and how she could get it as a teenager. Now here she was a mom.

Time kept moving. It was hard to believe. He would have been a dad too. He would have been a dad to a little girl. Lisa and he had not agreed on a name yet, but they had it down to Skylene Marie, or Alice Kayleen. Then they decided they would name her when she was born. They had nothing but time. She was just coming five months along. They had lots of time... He closed his eyes and shook his head, then stretched.

His dad wasn't up yet, so he could go for a quick run to clear his mind. The air felt good on his skin. He started off at an easy pace. The birds in the trees were babbling back and forth. Other than that, the only thing he heard was the rhythm of his feet and the sound of his breathing. He lost himself in the moment and let his legs find their pace. He turned up the old gravel road and kept his feet moving. His lungs screamed for air from the altitude change, but he kept running.

A young fork-horned buck in the velvet jumped from the side of the road, stood next to a tree, and watched him jog past. Craig looked at him for a moment, then returned his focus to the road. About a hundred yards down the dirt road, he veered off and just started running. He jumped a log, dodged a tree, and continued—no path, no guide or thought, just running to run. Over, through, around, dodging, ducking, and going. Climbing, climbing, over boulders, through buck brush and across the land he loved so much. Leaving behind the anguish of his past and trying to find a future. He was out of breath as he reached the top where there was a clearing. He stopped, put his hands on his hips and bent over to catch his breath. His shirt was soaked and clinging to him. He grabbed at it to pull it away from his body.

He looked up and saw the vast country around him. The openness and solitude of it all engulfed him. He turned and looked behind him and saw the rugged country that he had just covered. The road lay miles back, just a thin gray ribbon threaded through the mountains and trees. He thought for a moment and realized how he had been living his life. He was just like that ribbon of road below him, dodging and turning and running from what he thought he wanted. He found a rock and sat down. He surveyed the land and his life, how symbolic it was to be here at this place. He took his head in his hands and cried. Was it the climb? The altitude? The struggle? Craig didn't know, but whatever it was, he let the tears flow. Then he watched the sun as it kissed the mountains and brought light where there were shadows.

Paige held Libby at a nice lope as they crossed the open meadow into the wooded country. She wasn't going to go far, so she hadn't wanted a saddle. It just felt good to jump astride and be one with a horse for a while, and it had been quite some time since she had ridden Libby.

Working with her mother, drawing plans for ranches or private parties, took up more time than what she thought it would, but the income had been enough to allow her to buy her a little piece of property with a barn and a doublewide trailer that she had now. Sixteen acres, irrigation, pump, pond, and a quarter of a mile of driveway kept her busy. But right now it was about here and now and her horse. It seemed Libby was happy to go and see what she could see. Paige didn't want to follow a trail or get caught up with some hiker with llamas. She just wanted to ride and let Libby have her head as she picked her way around trees, logs, and branches. It felt good to be out and away for a while.

She had been gone a little over thirty minutes and thought it was time to start heading back toward the home. As they turned and started heading back, she again let her mind wander to all the things she had to do. Jim was going to pick up the mare and colt today. As she let Libby pick her way freely through the downed trees and shrubs, she felt her mind start lining up things that she needed to get done. She was so busy working with her mom, helping to design custom places and parks and landscapes, she was having a hard time keeping up with it all. Now having a teenage girl thrown into the mix as temporary foster care, Paige felt like life was moving too fast and she couldn't get everything done. Bills, checkbook, laundry, hay, feeding, work, house, and kid stuff. The list seemed endless.

Abby wasn't the same girl who had come to her four months ago, and Paige sure wasn't the same person either. For the first time since Abigail Sorensen showed up on her doorstep alone, angry and feeling abandoned, she looked like she was trying to find herself. Paige didn't know if she was the right person for the job, but on a temporary basis, she was getting the job done.

Abby had realized that she was not helpless and Paige understood she should not treat her as such. *Abby got around that mare alright this morning*, Paige thought. *Almost had a mishap, but she got it figured out and everything worked out ok.* And now they were actually having conversations. Paige knew she could not offer the city life to this girl, although it seemed that was where she wanted to go. So finding her a foster home closer to that style of living was probably the smart thing to do.

These random thoughts filtered through Paige's head as she continued to ride, allowing Libby to pick and choose her way through the beautiful timbered area. The sun was filtering through the trees, and the air was warm and pleasant, filled with the wildlife sounds of humming insects and timber squirrels.

Paige was so deep in thought that she paid no attention to the buzzing that was around her. She felt Libby tuck her tail then hump up. Paige felt a sting on her back, then one on her arm. Libby had stepped on a wasp's nest, and they were starting to swarm around them both. Paige nudged Libby forward as Libby started dancing around. She stepped on the nest again. Libby started to crow hop with her hind feet, and Paige urged her on. "Don't buck, baby, just go," she said. "Go!"

It was too late. Libby couldn't take any more of the angry wasps' stings on the underside of her belly. She took her head and hopped around, but Paige pushed her to go forward. More wasps were stinging Paige, and she fought them off her face. She took the reins and whopped Libby on the butt. "Go, baby, go!"

Libby lined out and headed through the trees. With that incentive, nothing was stopping her from getting out and away from those nasty wasps. Libby jumped a log and came out into a clearing. Wasps had gotten down

Paige's shirt and were biting and stinging her. She was trying to get her shirt off and slow Libby down, but Libby was running for her life.

Paige had her legs clamped around the barrel of her horse, and Libby's sides were sweaty and slick. Page started to slide to the side. Her hands were so busy trying to get the wasps off her, she couldn't grab hold of Libby's mane and fell in the tall grass in a heap. She felt the air leave her lungs in a wheeze.

Libby felt confused, scared, and naked without Paige astride her back. She slowed down to a trot and then a walk. She nickered and looked around trying to figure out what had just happened. She was alone. Paige was gone, hidden in the tall grass. Libby felt uncertain. She circled around and nickered again.

10

Craig was just coming out into the clearing where there was a little spring. He did a quick check for snakes before he squatted down and scooped up the cool water to splash on his face. He splashed it again and ran it back behind his neck. The coolness of the water took his breath away. It felt good. As he lifted his head to let the water run down his body, he heard something crashing through the trees. It sounded like a herd of elk.

Craig waited with bated breath in anticipation of seeing elk crashing into the clearing. It was something he had only heard about but had never seen. They were coming from the right. He listened and strained his eyes to see through the timber. He stood up and turned to get a better view, but what he saw was not a heard of elk. It was a lone golden palomino horse and rider, running bareback through the trees. The rider was acting really odd as he watched her, slapping herself and trying to stay on the stampeding horse. She fell to the side of the running horse in a heavy thud onto the ground.

The horse kept going, and Craig took off at a run to where the girl had landed. The golden horse circled and trotted around. Craig thought he recognized it, but that would be crazy. The girl was lying on her back, her blonde hair was covering her face. Craig looked at her arms. They had welts up and down them, and wasps were entangled in her hair. He tried to swat them away as he brushed her hair back. He saw six or seven wasp stings on her face and numerous ones on her neck. Paige Cason was lying before him unconscious. He heard a buzzing inside her shirt and realized she had more wasps all over her. He sat her up and pulled her shirt off her swollen, welted body.

He reached in his side pack and grabbed an Epi pen. The epinephrine was to help keep her air passage open. He didn't give a second thought to the fact that he was allergic and might get stung. With this many stings, he knew the best thing he could do was give her a shot in the thigh.

Paige lay motionless in his arms. He picked her limp body up and headed toward the spring. "Paige, can you hear me? Paige?" There was no response. "Don't you die on me, Paige, you hear me? Don't you dare die on me." Panic was in his voice. *Keep my head,* he thought, *focus on what I know.* "Paige?" His voice was concerned yet demanding.

Libby wanted to follow. She was lost on what to do. Her instincts were to be with people, but she found nothing familiar about the strange man who came running out of the trees. She trotted about five strides in the direction of home, then looked back toward the girl she had trusted almost her entire life. She circled around, looking for familiarity, a hint of something that would help her make the choice of going home alone or staying. She again looked in the distance toward home and safety then back at the man carrying her owner. She really didn't want to be alone. When that choice was made, there was no turning back.

Craig remembered when they were kids and Paige would give a silly little whistle to make Libby come running. He thought of giving it a try, but then if she ran home maybe someone would come and start looking for her. How long would it take for someone to find them?

He thought of how she whistled and tried to imitate it, but his mouth was dry and only air came out. He had to keep moving. He licked his lips and gave another try. Four little bursts of air through the tongue and roof of his mouth.

Libby lifted her head in recognition, then instantly came at a lope. Her choice was made.

Craig got Paige to the spring and started dabbing mud on her wasp stings. There were too many to count, so he carefully laid her in the mud, grabbed handfuls, and started packing her body with it. Her face was swollen, but her airway seemed to be open. He caked mud on her neck and back, on her cheeks, and then down her chest, across her belly and below her belt line. "Oh, God, please forgive me," he mumbled as he undid her pants and saw the sting bites as he pulled them down, swiping more wasps that had flown up her pant legs. "Paige. Come on, Paige. I need to know you are going to be alright. He got her pants off and coated her legs with mud, adding more water to dirt. She was burning up. He knew he had to make a mad dash to his house. Libby stood there waiting. She was ready to ride.

"Little lady, do you think you can help me out here?" Craig asked as he looked at the horse with welts all over her body too. "Easy, babe. Easy," he said as he reached for her rein. "Paige, I am going to borrow your horse for a minute. If you can, stay close to the water. Paige, can you hear me? Stay in the mud and I will be back as soon as I can."

He stroked Libby's neck and jumped astride. His bigger frame made her snap to attention and surge forward.

"Alright, little lady, let's go." He nudged her forward, and she responded with such power and strength that it caught Craig off guard. He was jolted back toward her flanks and had to grab her mane to pull himself up behind her withers until he adjusted to the power and speed of her lurching forward. He wrapped his legs around her ribs, found her rhythm, and let her carry him.

They were over four miles from his house. He thought of how he would run and let her find her own stride. He pulled up on the rein to let her know she needed to conserve her energy and not waste it on a sprint. Libby found the rhythm with her breathing. She sounded like a freight train, taking air in short bursts and exhaling with the rhythm of her feet. Craig relaxed and gave her permission to do what she needed to do. It had been years since he had felt that kind of power beneath him, and it made him wonder how he had survived without a horse. The rhythm and power meshed together with heart and wind.

"Come on, Libby, you are doing great," he said as he hit the paved road heading toward his dad's house. "Another half mile to go. Please, God, I beg you. Help me get Paige help," he whispered under his breath. "Don't let her die."

He rode up in front of his dad's house. Jim was sitting on the porch with some coffee. "What is going on, Craig?" Jim asked as he noticed the strange lathered golden mare that Craig was riding.

"Paige rode into a wasp's nest and is stung so many times I can't count. She is up by the little spring. Call an ambulance, Dad. I will grab the jeep!" He trotted Libby into the barn and out to the back corral. He pulled off her bridle and shut the gate.

"Call Abe and Patricia. You can meet me at the hospital." Craig grabbed water, some Benadryl, and a blanket and jumped into his old jeep. "She is unconscious, Dad. Have them head my direction, and I will be on my way in with her."

Craig said all of this while he was in motion. He threw everything in the back of the Jeep and started the engine to head back the same way he came.

Jim was on his feet and making phone calls. He didn't know for sure what was happening, but he heard the concern in his son's voice and knew it was serious. 9-1-1, little spring, lots of wasp stings, Paige, ambulance, and Abe and Patricia.

Jim heard someone answer the phone, "9-1-1, what is your emergency?"

Craig cut off the road and drove across the little meadow to the spring where he had left Paige. He pulled up beside her and could hear that she was trying to talk. Her throat was raspy, and she was having a hard time getting air. Her eyes were swollen shut, and her face looked like someone had hit her with a bat.

"Don't talk, Paige," he whispered to her. "You are going to be alright."

Paige tried to say something again, so he put his ear down to her mouth. "What, Paige?"

"Abby," she whispered.

"Libby?" He guessed. He tried to explain, "She is at the house. I put her in a corral and will check on her when we get you to the hospital."

"No, Abby," she whispered. Why couldn't she get the voice out? She could hear herself say it, but it was not coming out the way she wanted.

He caked her again with mud. "Here, drink some water." He put a bottle of water up to her lips to dampen them and she coughed. Craig put down the water and grabbed his blanket. He carefully lifted her and wrapped her in it.

"Abby," she said again, barely coherent.

"I will check on her. You just rest now. Alright?" He slipped her small frame into the passenger side of the jeep and buckled her in. He jumped into the driver's side and started toward the road.

"Paige?" he said, but there was no response. "Paige?" he said it louder. "Don't you die on me!" he demanded. "Don't you dare die on me."

He made it to the road and floored it. Dust billowed up from behind while he kept his eyes on the road. He turned onto the highway and shifted into fifth gear. He picked his speed up to seventy-five miles an hour and turned on his flashers. Paige's head was cocked to the side and the wind was blowing her hair.

He had to say something. He had to keep talking to her, so he started to ramble.

"Remember at the horse show when you cussed out Samantha Greenly? Do you remember that day, Paige?" he said with a fake laugh, memories flooded his mind. "I remember how determined you were. You were like a pistol." He thought a little bit. "How about when I brought your awards out and ended up spending the whole day at your house with you and your family? That was one of the best days, one of my best memories." He paused a moment again, thinking. "How about that night, before your mom took me home. Do you remember that I kissed you?" His voice trailed off. "That is a moment I will never forget, Paige. I had to summon up a lot of courage, but I was afraid you wouldn't know what I was feeling. Do you remember?" he rambled. Then he thought again of what they had done together. "How about your birthday party? That one where I surprised you." He smiled. "You were so surprised you dropped all that soda." He grinned as he thought of it. "We have had some times, Paige, you and I. We have good memories."

He looked at her and realized she wasn't coherent. "Paige, can you hear me? You got to stick with me, babe. You hear me? You have got to stick with me." His hands started shaking, and he felt sobs come from his mouth. "Paige, we are going for help, so stay with me alright?" He felt a tear run down his cheek. "I am right here and we have an ambulance on the way." He reached over, took her hand, and gave it a squeeze. He felt her give a little squeeze back, then her hand went limp.

He topped the little rise and saw the ambulance lights. He pulled into a wide spot, skidding in the gravel, and jumped out of the jeep to flag them down.

One of the EMTs jumped out of the ambulance, headed to the passenger side of the jeep, and began evaluating Paige. The other emergency responders positioned the ambulance and prepared for transport.

"What happened?" the first EMT asked as he took her pulse.

"I don't know for sure, but I think her horse stepped on a wasp's nest. She was covered in wasps when I got to her. She fell off her horse and hit pretty hard. I gave her my epinephrine shot, then took her over to the spring and put mud on her to kind of help with the burning."

The first EMT listened as the other two were getting the gurney ready. He was trying to get her pulse and wiping away the dried mud on her arm. They moved swiftly and started reading off pulse, blood pressure, and other vital signs. They immediately put an IV in her arm and got her on the gurney.

"We will take it from here," the lead EMT said. "Come on to the hospital." As they pushed her into the ambulance, he noticed Craig following and not wanting to leave Paige's side. "If you want to ride with us you can, but it would be wise to bring your rig in. Let's load up," he said as they shut the door.

Craig ran his hand through his hair. A feeling of loss, anxiety, and helplessness filled his heart once again. He wiped tears from his eyes and shoved the anguish aside. He was going to see this through. He jumped into the jeep and followed them in.

11

Abby sat on the porch. She had read two books and thought she might be getting the idea of what cutting horses were all about. She was getting a little nervous because usually when Paige said she wouldn't be long, she was about a half hour to forty-five minutes. Now it was going on three hours. Still no sign. She had tried calling Mr. and Mrs. Cason, but nobody answered. She would just wait awhile.

She looked out at Cougar and the mare. Cougar was sleeping lazily under the shade tree, his little tail flopping back and forth in an effort to scare off flies. In all actuality, it looked like a little mop head flopping back and forth. His golden hide glistened in the sun. He didn't even look like the same baby that was buried in the mud five days ago. He looked bigger, stronger, and feistier than what he had been that day. She thought about what would have happened had she not gone for a walk that day and about how Paige talked of making decisions. It seemed right. She had been on the negative side and she was starting to understand that by doing one thing or making one choice, she could change her whole life around. She smiled.

There was a black jeep pulling up in the driveway. It was a rig she had not seen before. She stood up and watched it pull in. Blue got up and went to the gate. She barked a couple of times then wagged her stubby tail. Craig sat in the jeep and looked at Abby.

"Hey, are you Abby?" He smiled at her.

His face looked familiar to her. "Yeah," she answered.

"My name is Craig Curry. My dad is Jim Curry. You saved his colt that got stuck in the mud."

Craig stayed in the jeep and leaned on his steering wheel. "Can you do me a favor, Abby? I want you to go in and call this number. It is my dad's cell phone, and you'll ask to talk to Patricia Cason. Can you do that for me?"

He gave her the phone number and then she asked, "Why?"

"Paige has been in an accident and I came out to get you. But I don't want to take you anywhere until you talk to Jim, Patricia, and Abe. Alright?"

It had sounded like a good idea at the time when he offered to go get her, just because he wanted to get out of the hospital and do something besides sit there and wait. But now that he was here, he sure didn't want to scare this girl.

She looked at him again and said, "I know you."

Craig looked surprised. "No, I don't think you do. I just came home to visit for a while," he said with a half grin on his face.

"Yes, I do, you are that guy in the picture," she said triumphantly.

"What picture is that?" he questioned, now curious of what she had seen.

She went into the house and got his senior picture out of the photo album. She looked at it again. She knew for a fact that was him.

She ran out of the house and Craig was standing at the gate. She handed it to him.

He chuckled as he looked at the younger him and read the inscription. "Yep, that is me alright," he said as he handed her back the baby-faced boy in the letterman jacket.

"Why don't you call them anyways, just to talk to them, and I will wait right here." He gave her the number again and watched her disappear back into the house. He walked over to the paddock and saw the mare standing lazily under the shade tree. The baby was flapping his little tail back and forth while he napped.

Abby came out of the house with a cordless phone. "Yes, Mrs. Cason, he is right here. Hold on." She walked out and handed the phone over the fence. "She wants to talk to you."

"Hi, Mrs. Cason, I mean Patricia," he stumbled. "Yeah, I can bring her right in. We will do chores here before we come in. Everything will be taken care of. She is stable? Good. Yep." He paused. "Yep I will have her pack a few things. Thanks. Yep let me put her back on."

"Back to you, little sister," he said with a grin.

Abby said, "Hello." she paused. "Alright." She listened. "Yep. Ok, I will. Ok. See you in a little while. Bye."

Abby looked at Craig. "Do you want to help me do chores?"

"Sure, I would love to help you."

She opened the gate and crutched her way down to the barn.

"Is this the mare I was supposed to pick up today?" he asked as he altered his steps to match hers.

"Yeah, I guess. Mr. Curry was going to come and get them. I call him Cougar." She said it halfheartedly. "Just because of what he went through and lived to tell about it." She repeated what Tom, the vet, had said earlier.

Then she blurted it out. "Is Paige going to die?"

He looked at her. "No, they got her stable, but she has been stung by a lot of wasps and she will be in pretty tough shape for the next couple of days."

"Where is Libby?" she asked as tears started to roll down her face.

She is at my dad's house right now. I rode her down there to get help for Paige."

They got to the barn, Abby remembered the routine that Paige had always done and followed it like protocol. She put grain in the bucket before crutching her way through the gate.

"What do you need me to do?" Craig asked.

"Well." She thought of the chores she had done. "If you could, get a couple of flakes of hay and put it in the mangers, one for each horse."

"Alright," Craig said as he cut a three-string bale of grass hay.

Abby went back through the gate and then whistled just like Paige. The horses lifted their heads and started coming in. She waited in silence as the horses trotted through the open corral gate. When everyone was settled, she hobbled through, crossed the corral, and shut the gate to lock them in for the night.

Craig watched and said nothing. "Now the challenging one," she said with a sigh. "I did this for the first time this morning. And I am going to do it again." She went and got the rope halter and walked out to the mare and colt. She crutched out across the paddock and tried to get the halter ready for the mare. The mare waited as Abby untied the halter and again looked at all the holes trying to figure out which one the nose went in.

"Need any help?" Craig asked.

"If I could just figure out which one is the nose hole, I could make this thing work," Abby said exasperated.

"I can show you a trick," Craig stated as he walked across the paddock. The mare raised her head and looked at him.

"Easy, lady," he said as he approached.

Abby was embarrassed. "I know I can get it once I figure it out."

"Oh, I know you can get it. There is no doubt in my mind. I will just help you find it, so you can work it out for yourself. See this line here? That goes under the jaw," Craig said as he ran his hand down the rope halter. "There are cheek holes here and here, on each side. This part, here," he continued, "goes over the head like that, right behind the ears," he said quietly as he slipped it on the mare's head to show Abby how it went. Then just as quietly, he asked, "Do you got it?"

"Yes."

"Good." Then he slipped the halter off the mare's head and gave it back to Abby. He turned to walk away.

"Hey!" she said. "What did you do that for? You had her caught."

"I know, but you're the one who wanted to catch her," he said teasingly as he waited by the gate.

Abby looked at the halter and the line that went down the underside of the jaw. She brought her hand up over the horse's neck and her nose just fell into the halter. "Hey, Craig, that works!"

Craig grinned at her.

Abby resituated her crutches and got her lead line in her left hand. She took a breath and looked at the gate, then at the napping Cougar lying in the shade. "Come on, sweet pea," she said as she started crutching her way to the gate. The mare followed willingly.

Cougar raised his head, got up, and stretched his legs and arched his neck, like he had just gotten up from a wonderful nap. He watched his mom leaving for a moment then trotted up beside her. He seemed happy to walk alongside her for a moment, then as if hunger had gotten from his tummy to his brain, he trotted in front of her to stop so he could nurse.

Abby didn't stop nor did the mare even make an effort to stop. So he again tried to stop his mom by stepping in front and stopping. Again he failed in the attempt to nurse. He pinned back his ears and kicked up his hind feet, shaking his head as he trotted in front of her again.

Craig noticed the efforts made by the little guy and had to laugh. "I think this little guy has a temper. He sure doesn't take no for an answer."

"Yeah, he is a tough one." She smiled at him.

She crutched her way to the barn and put them in the larger stall. Cougar was still pouting at not getting his milk when he wanted, so he walked in the stall quietly. As Abby pulled off the halter, Cougar started to nurse.

"We just put them in here for safety at night. Blue is pretty good about letting us know if we have company.

The cougar hasn't been back since she ran it off," Abby told him as she latched the stall door.

"Well looks like we are going to have to do some horse trading in the next couple of days," Craig said as Abby started to walk toward him.

He admired this young girl and her will to get things done.

"Now all I have to do is water," she said as she started heading toward the faucet.

"Why don't I water and you go ahead and get your things packed for a couple of days."

Abby looked at him. "Alright, there are four water troughs to fill," she said as she lifted her crutches and headed to the house.

The mare and foal had a full manger of hay and a fifty-gallon water trough that was divided between two stalls. This mare was the only one in the barn, so there were no concerns for her.

He walked out and found two more water troughs where the horses were in the corral, then he found one out in the pasture just behind the house. He filled them all up and was done just as Abby walked out of the house.

"What are we supposed to do with Blue?" she asked concerned as shut the house door, then she looked at Craig.

"Well I would say bring her along. No sense in being here by herself."

Abby grinned. "Come on, Blue."

Blue jumped in the front seat then settled in the back of the jeep. She was anxious to go.

He stepped into the Jeep and started it up. Since there were no doors, Abby struggled a little to get in and slipped her crutches into the backseat. She then cinched down her seatbelt and grabbed the roll bar.

"Don't worry, Abby, I won't be crazy," he said with a grin as he revved his engine a few times before putting it in gear and heading down the driveway for town.

12

Paige couldn't speak. She tried but nothing seemed to be coming out of her mouth. She saw a man. He looked familiar, but she couldn't think of who he was. Her body seemed be on fire. Her legs couldn't move. Someone was carrying her. Holding her. She could hear a voice, a nice voice. It was calling her name. Why did she know that voice? She felt secure and safe as the arms wrapped around her. She could feel his heart beat through his shirt.

That was weird, she thought, her mind was foggy. *Who was dying? Nobody should be dying. She was right here. Couldn't he see her?* The fire on her skin was deeper now. *God could someone put out the fire?* Her mouth was dry, "Water," she said, "water." But no one could hear her. "Please water." She tried to move her mouth, yet nothing would happen. She could hear someone whistle. Who was whistling? *Was that me?* she thought. *Sounds like me whistling.* She heard horse hooves hitting the ground at a lope. She couldn't open her eyes.

I am so hot. I feel like I am on fire, she tried to say. She heard a moan. *Was that me?*

Then coolness…the feeling of something cool on her skin and more being rubbed on her like a thick paste, cool and refreshing.

Water. She couldn't reach it. Her mouth was so dry. She heard someone pray. *That is a good idea*, she thought. I will pray too. *What should I pray for?* She thought for a moment. She thought of making the burning go away, and then she prayed for Abby, the lost soul of a child who needed a family to be a part of.

The thick stuff felt good on her face around her eyes, on her neck. *Why do they keep calling me?* she thought. *I am right here. Can't you see me? Look right here.*

She heard a horse coming. Libby crossed her mind. "Libby," she tried to say to let her know she was ok.

Then someone was saying goodbye. "No, don't leave. Don't leave me here. I want to go too." She tried to move her arms, but they wouldn't work. Paige tried to wave them back but the thundering sound of horse hooves faded away. The coolness of the mud relaxed her. She wasn't burning anymore. She was so tired. She just wanted to sleep for now.

***

Paige could hear the hustle of people running back and forth. Her arms and legs were too heavy for her to lift. She heard her dad's voice, and Abe Cason walked into the room.

"Hey, Sis. Looks like you got yourself in a fix." He took her swollen hand and held it. "Just want you to know that we are here. Alright?" His voice sounded choked up.

Then she heard her mom's voice. "Hey, Paige, we are right here." She pulled up a chair, and it scratched across the floor.

"Could someone please untie my hands? I can't move my hands." She tried to speak but nothing seemed work— her voice or her mouth. She tried again. *Why can't they hear me?*

She heard a soft beep, beep, beep. Where was she? She felt really tired and thought she would rest for a while. She would make sense of it all later. Her mind was quiet again.

13

Abe and Patricia Cason had been working hard to pull together their little ranch. Abe had the little stud he called Shorty because of his size that had turned out to be a dandy sire. He was producing cutting horses. With Poco Lena and Gun Smoke on his papers, Shorty knew how to place his feet and was small and agile enough to get down eye to eye with a cow. Abe had been gone for the last week working part of the circuit with a couple of nice horses, but the one he loved to put in front of a cow was Shorty.

He had gotten home the night before and had unloaded his horses. He put Shorty out in his little pasture with his pasture buddy, a donkey called Chance. Shorty was never mean to Chance, but they did like to play and keep each other company when Shorty was home. Shorty walked over to the water and took a deep drink. Then he walked away, turned a few circles, buckled his knees, and laid down to roll. He rubbed his head up and down, making sure his mane was getting a good dose of dirt. He was tired of being a clean horse. Now he wanted to have a dust bath.

He rolled around a time or two then got up and gave himself a good shake. Dust flew in all directions. Chance came over, lay down next to him and did the same thing. Rubbing his head up and down and dropping to his knees rolling in the same manner, his long coarse hair holding most of the dirt, not shaking near like Shorty's did.

Abe took his two geldings out next and turned them out in the back pasture. They had done well for their first time out. Abe was pleased. He went and turned on the hose and watched them stroll around a little while before they too dropped and rolled. *It must feel good,* Abe thought.

He felt a hand come up around his waist and his wife's head laid in the middle of his back.

"Hey, babe, welcome home," Patricia said as she squeezed him and breathed in his smell.

Abe turned to look at her and cupped her chin in his hands. She looked at him. "It is good to be home," he said as he leaned down and gave her a kiss. He held her a moment and stroked her hair as they looked out at the two geldings grazing on pasture grass.

"Good trip?" she asked.

"A real good trip," he answered. "Was a long one but I think it was a good one. Winnemucca is a good place to go," he said. "There are a couple of guys who want to cover their mares with Shorty. I am also going to pick up a couple more colts to work from a ranch down at Battle Mountain. So looks like I will have plenty to do.

"What about you?" He looked at Patricia. "What has been going on here?"

"Well, let's see." She sighed. "Got two more contracts for barn plans and one more for designing three different parks. Looks like that will take me the rest of the summer. My garden is weeded, the horses are fed, and there is supper waiting to be eaten." She took his hand and swung it back and forth as if they were school kids.

"Say no more. I think I could eat a horse." He smiled at her and gave her a kiss. Then they walked to the house.

"Have you heard anything from Paige?" he asked as he dried his hands and walked to the kitchen table.

"Not in the last couple of days. She has been working pretty hard on a project she took on. I think it is coming along pretty well, but she hasn't shared it with me yet." Patricia folded the towel and put it on the oven door. "Paige said Abby is doing pretty well, but boy I think she bit off more than she can chew, having that young girl stay with her and trying to make a living." Patricia paused, "Boy, Abe, I don't know how anyone can get over the hump of losing both parents." She looked at her husband for a moment and then realized he had the same thing happen to him.

He had never said anything about it, but he probably knew exactly what that girl might be feeling.

"I have been doing a lot of thinking about Abby, and I think that little girl is in the right place. It is kind of odd how she got here and how Paige ended up with her, but at least she is in a home that might help her find her place. Sometimes it feels like silent whispers come into our lives. I sure hope that if she is meant to be here she is able to stay here," Abe stated.

"I just worry about her sometimes," Patricia continued. "The girl is so withdrawn and nothing seems to bring her out of her shell. Although the other day, Paige called and said that they had a cougar chase one of Jim Curry's colts into Paige's spring. Abby was the one who got it out while Paige was in town. I can't wait to hear the whole story. That little girl can barely get around let alone help a colt out of a bog. She has got to have heart, that one does."

"How about we go over and see them tomorrow and see what they have been up to."

"Sounds good to me," Patricia said as she sat down at the table.

Abe bowed his head as they held hands and said grace.

"Lord, if there is a better day than this, please let it be lived and appreciated. As for now, we thank you for this day and the food we share. Now let us privately say our peace."

Silence filled the room for a moment, then he squeezed Patricia's hand, looked into her eyes, and held her gaze.

"I love you, Patricia Cason," he said with a sigh.

"I love you too, Abe Cason." She smiled at him. "Boy it is good to have you home." She put a hand on his leg and patted it, then reached for her fork.

14

Craig and Abby got to the hospital. Abby looked over at Blue and got worried. "Blue, you stay," she said, realizing there was no way to keep her in the jeep.

Blue sat down and watched them get out. She watched as the automatic doors opened and some people exited the facility. Blue smelled the air for a moment then whined. Without a second thought, she jumped out of the jeep just as Craig and Abby made it almost all the way to the doors. A flash of Blue came racing up between them, running through the open doors and down the hallway.

She trotted past the nurses and doctors and searched for one person. She got halfway down one hall before she turned and backtracked. Then she headed down another hall and stopped at a door in ICU. She jumped up on the window and looked in. Patricia saw Blue, while Craig and Abby were close on her trail. Blue went to the door and pushed it with her paw, got her nose pushed through, and walked in the room. She put her feet up on the bed and whined. She touched her nose to Paige's swollen hand, but there was no response. Blue again pushed her nose against it. Standing on her hind legs, she attempted again to get Paige's attention. Then she waited. With front paws on the bed, she laid her head next to Paige's hand.

Abby and Craig came around the corner. Neither one of them had known what to expect. Paige had a tube down her throat and an IV in her arm. The heart monitor was beeping in the background. Patricia and Abe were sitting next to her. Jim came up next to him and put his hand on Craig's shoulder.

"No change," Jim said as he looked over at Abby.

"Is that her?" she asked quietly.

"Yes. She is just swollen with all the stings. They say that will go down in a day or so. Don't you worry, she will be as good as new in a few days."

Patricia came out of the room. "Hi, Abby." She could see the shock on the girl's face.

Abby looked at Patricia. She felt lightheaded. Her legs began to feel weak and started shaking. She had to get out of there! She was not going to go through another death. Life was unfair, and death was cruel! She just couldn't take it. She spun around and started to run, dropping her crutches.

She ran blindly, her legs wanting to buckle under her, but she forced them to keep moving. Incoherent, she couldn't find the door, and she staggered from one hallway to the other dragging her bad leg. Searching, not seeing, not hearing. All she thought was good was a lie. Tears blurred her vision. She found the door and burst through. She crumpled on the lawn and couldn't breathe, sobs were coming from her throat, and she couldn't stop them. She struggled on the uneven ground. She tried to get up but her legs would not work. They acted like they were tied in knots. She buried her head and cried.

Abe and Craig both went after her, one went down one hallway and the other down another. Abe found her going out the door. He jogged after her. "Abby," he said hoping she would hear him, but she kept going. He got out the door and found her small frame of a body sobbing on the ground. She tried to get up, but her legs wouldn't work. His heart broke in two. He laid the crutches down, then sat down next to her head and waited. Every now and again, he would stroke her auburn hair just letting her know that she was not alone.

"She can't die," she sobbed. "She just can't die."

Abe touched her shoulder as she cried. "I don't think

she is going to die, Abby. She is just hurting so much they gave her something to get rid of the pain. That's all."

She looked at him for a moment. "She is going to make it?"

"Yes, I believe so." Abe replied, trying to keep his voice even. Craig came out of the doors and walked over to where they sat. "Do you mind if I have a seat too?" he said as he sat on the other side of her.

Then Patricia came out also. "Abby, are you ok?" she asked as she also sat down in the grass.

Abby looked at her, then at Abe and then at Craig. "She is going to be alright?" she asked again.

Patricia brushed Abby's hair away from her tear-streaked face. "They are doing everything possible for her. The outlook is good though. Why don't we give it a couple of days and see how it looks from there." Patricia brushed one of the tears off Abby's cheek. "Let's give her a chance to heal."

Craig looked over at Abe and said, "Well, I will be in town for a couple of weeks. I can take care of Paige's place." He said it boldly like that was what he was supposed to do.

"Abby," Patricia said. "Abe and I want you to come and stay with us. At least until Paige gets to feeling better."

Abby looked at each one again and realized they were doing what Paige had explained earlier that day. They were making choices to make good out of what happened. "I would like to stay with you, Mrs. Cason. Can Blue come too?"

"Blue is always welcome at our place," Patricia said with love and affection. "Just as you are always welcome at our place."

Abby smiled. Some of the aloneness lifted from her broken heart. She had the strength to help out and be a part of a family. She reached over and wrapped her arms around Patricia and put her head on her shoulder. Patricia closed her eyes, held her, and rocked her back and forth like a child that had been lost but now found.

For once since the accident, Abby let herself relax and be held. She had resisted all contact with anything that might cause her to care. Through the pain and anguish, through the foster system, the physical therapy, it seemed that everyone had been poking and prodding on her. It didn't seem anyone could understand. But now she was the one who was beginning to understand. She was afraid it could all be taken away and she had nothing left to give. Yet in that moment when she felt Patricia wrap her arms around her and felt the comfort of motherly love, she let tears flow. Anguish released and a feeling of love filled her up.

Both Abe and Craig got up and walked back inside the hospital. They found Jim in the waiting room. They all three sat together and started making a plan to get everything done.

"The doctor said Paige will sleep through the night. She should be a little more coherent tomorrow, and she should be out in a day or so. They are going to keep her sedated until some of that poison gets out of her system."

"It was a good thing you had an Epi pen and some Benadryl with you, Craig. They think that saved her life."

They shuffled around times and shifts so that there was always someone with Paige.

Craig volunteered first. He could stay with her tonight since all her chores were done and Abby had had a pretty big day. "I will call you if there are any changes or problems."

Blue was lying under the bed. She could no longer stand next to Paige. Abby called her, "Come on, Blue. Come on, girl." Blue raised her head and looked at the girl then dropped her head back to the floor. She wasn't leaving tonight.

"I will watch her, Abbs," Craig said. The nurses said she could stay since there are no other patients in the room.

Abby looked at him. That was what Paige always called her, and it used to drive her nuts. She had tried to correct Paige several times but to no avail. And now it was almost like it belonged to her. Her life was changing.

15

The day after Paige's accident, Abby went out to watch Abe work one of the geldings in a round pen. She sat and watched him ride over to the fence, open the gate then head out into the pasture. He loped a couple of circles, brought the horse to a stop, and with a slight touch of hand and tilt of shoulder the horse started spinning in a circle again. Abby watched, mesmerized in the moment of horse and person being one.

"How do you do that?" she asked him as he rode back a little while later.

"Do what?" Abe replied.

"Make that horse do all those things?"

"What things?" Abe was curious what caught Abby's attention.

"Turn in circles and back up and stuff," she asked kind of frustrated because she didn't know how to say what she was wanting to know.

Abe stroked the bay gelding's neck then stepped off as smooth as water. "I don't make him do anything, Abby. I just suggest what I want and get out of his way. He just kind of knows."

"How does he know?"

"Because we do a lot of talking, him and me," Abe answered as he moved the stirrup and loosened the cinch.

"Like I talk to Blue?"

"No, there are a lot of different ways to communicate and with horses, it is a silent talk."

"What do you mean silent talk?"

"When you go out to feed the horses, do you notice the horses move and shift around until they get where they need to be."

"Well yeah."

"That is silent talk. Every action means something to them, just like every word means something to you. They know where they stand in the pecking order with the horses around them and are able to do what makes them comfortable. I have spent a lifetime learning how to listen to them. I don't always get it right, but I am getting better every day."

Abby was almost lost in the conversation, but she tried to understand.

"Do you think I might be able to do that some day?"

"Well you already communicate with the horses, so I know you are able," Abe stated.

"What do you mean I communicate with them?" Abby seemed a little more confused.

Abe looked at his horse. "Tell me what Cricket is thinking. Look at his body language and tell me. Is he scared, excited, happy, bored?"

Abby looked at the gelding, "I don't know," she paused and looked at him like seeing him for the first time. She noticed his ear was turned toward Abe, his eyes were soft and not wild looking, yet he wasn't sleeping either. His head was a little over waist high to Abe. "He looks content."

"How do you know that?" Abe asked to make his point.

"I don't know. He just seems that way. I guess because he has his ear cocked toward you, and he seems happy next to you."

"I would agree with you," Abe said as he stroked Cricket's neck. "The thing is, with a horse we have to go by feel. We can tell a dog good boy and they wag their tail. A horse is more subtle, you already have recognized that. That is the communication I am talking about." Abe paused. "So if you want to learn more, you are more than capable to. It just depends on how bad you want it. But yeah, I think you can do anything you set your mind to."

"Even with my leg and all?"

"Well, Abby," Abe said matter-of-factly. "If you want to blame your leg for not riding, that is fine with me, but I have seen people in wheelchairs ride horses."

"So you think I can ride?"

"I know you can ride, but it is not up to me. The choice is up to you."

Abby was silent. "Did you teach Paige to ride too?"

"I supported Paige in riding yes. She listened to what I had to say and is amazing on a horse. I can only teach you what you want to learn, the rest of it is up to you." Abe watched her for a moment as she tried to piece things together. "It is like anything you learn Abby, you learn what you want to learn. In school you have teachers who teach you, but you choose what you learn."

Abby raised an eyebrow. "I hate math. It is so hard."

"So you choose not to learn math. You can only learn what you want. You can blame it on the teacher, or the school, heck you can blame it on the problem. But the fact is when you really want something, and I mean really want it, you figure it out. For instance how long did it take for you to learn how to walk?"

Abby looked confused, "I don't know."

"Did you just get up one day and say, 'Today I am going to walk,' and walk across the kitchen? Or did you fall down, scoot around, get back up and try again? Or did you just give up and never learn?" Abe smiled. "Did you say, 'This walking thing is too hard, so I ain't even gonna try anymore. I will just scoot around on my butt the rest of my life.'?"

Abby smiled at the thought for a moment as her head spun with how many times she wanted to give up and how hard it had been to keep going forward.

Abe continued, "You figure it out no matter how hard you have to try or what obstacles you have to go through. For instance think of something you really wanted."

Abby said, "My cell phone."

"What did you have to do to get it?"

Abby smiled remembering when her mother bribed her with the dishes. "I had to do the dishes for a week."

"When you got it," Abe continued, "did you know how to work it?"

"No, it took me a couple of days to figure it out." Abby thought back.

"Were you frustrated? Did you get angry? Did you figure it out or did you just give up and throw it away?"

"No, I got frustrated, but I wouldn't throw it away! I loved my phone."

"So you learned to use your phone no matter how hard it was."

Abby smiled as realization struck her. "I will get good at the things I work at."

"There is no obstacle you cannot overcome, Abby. It is a question of how bad do you want it and what you are going to do about it," Abe said as he walked to the barn with Cricket to unsaddle him.

Abby watched him walk away and thought long and hard about what Abe was saying.

"Mr. Cason," Abby said boldly, crutching her way after him. "I want to learn how to ride."

"Well then let's see if we can help you out with that." Abe smiled. "So that means you are going to have to do a little work around here to get your strength up. Are you up for that?"

"What do you want me to do?"

"What can you do?"

Abby looked at him a moment and thought of how to answer. "I can lead horses. I can brush them, grain and feed them." Abby thought again, trying to come up with other things she could do.

"That is a good start," Abe stated. "So let's look at starting this afternoon and then with chores."

Abby beamed.

Later that day, Abe asked Abby, "Why don't you catch Cricket and brush him out for me?"

Abby's heart skipped a beat. "Alright," she said as her mind raced with how to put on the halter.

Abe reached out and handed her a rope halter just like the one Paige had. She took it from him cautiously, just as he had handed it to her. She noticed that the nosepiece stuck out a little from the rest of the halter and the line that went under the jaw was behind the nosepiece, just like Craig had said. She walked to the stall and slid open the gate. Cricket stood quietly as Abby presented the halter to him. He dropped his nose in and waited for it to be tied. Abby let her breath out. The gelding did the same as the pair walked out of the stall.

Abe handed her a brush. "Use this one. When you are done, take him out to the pasture with the other horses."

"Okay," Abby said as she took the brush and looked back at Cricket. She thought of how she had seen Paige brush Libby and began with the head. Cricket seemed pleased as she stroked his neck and down his back. As she stroked his hide, she felt a calmness come over her. She saw and felt him breathe in and out, the warmth of his body. She saw his heartbeat pulsing in his veins. She lost herself in brushing stokes and feeling until his coat was smooth and glossy. She noticed the funny looking hair laying the wrong way on his flank and how the mane was long, thick and silky soft. She felt like she wanted to braid it. Abby forgot time and history. She immersed herself in feeling.

When she had finished brushing Cricket, Abe challenged her with cleaning a couple of stalls and checking the horses' water. She had found a little pull wagon and used it to her advantage. Taking a few hay strings, she braided them together and tied them to the handle. She used it for a sling over her shoulder so she could haul hay and put buckets of water on the wagon to fill the stall water trough and still use her crutches.

She kept asking herself, "If I could do this, how would I get it done?"

Patricia looked out the window and saw how innovative Abby was with the wagon. She smiled to herself. *What an amazing girl she is,* she thought as she turned back to her work in her office.

When Abe got in to the house that night, he felt that Abby was true to her ambitions. He made a call to John Greenly.

"Hey, John, I was wondering if you still had Piper."

John Greenly sat and listened to Abe on the other end of the phone sketch out his plan to help a young girl learn to ride.

"Abe, I think Piper would love to work. He has been out here in the pasture for the last couple of years."

"Well I sure would appreciate it, John."

"I will bring him out tomorrow," John said. "I am happy to help."

That night at the dinner table, Abby told Patricia and Abe about reading the books at Paige's place and how amazing cutting horses seemed to be. How she watched Paige jump on Libby without a saddle and how Libby turned without Paige even using the reins. They were connected or something and they had just ridden off. The only time Abby had been on a horse was when they went to a dude ranch and rode one of their trail horses when she was a girl. How she really had to pull on the horse to get it to turn or do anything at all.

Patricia and Abe both smiled, listening to the excitement come from her.

"Well," Patricia said, "let's see if we can change that."

***

The following morning John Greenly pulled up with a white horse trailer in tow. Abe heard the truck and called to Abby. "Hey, Abby, I have someone here I want you to meet."

Abby took off her shoulder sling to her wagon and came out of the barn. She had no idea what was happening but was excited to see a horse trailer. She crutched her way beside Abe as he went out to greet John.

"Morning, John."

"Hey, Abe."

"John, I would like you to meet Abigail Sorenson. She has been staying with Paige for the last few months."

"Nice to meet you, Abigail," John said as he held out his hand. "So you're the girl who wants to learn to ride."

"Yeah, Mr. Cason said that I can if I set my mind to it," Abby said, trying to be confident in the conversation.

"Well," John said, "he is right. You have to want to first."

"I want to, more than anything."

John looked at the girl with her crutches under her arms. He thought of ten years prior when his own daughter, Samantha, was in her position. "You know, Abigail, if you listen to this man and horses are what you want to do, you will be a success."

Abby had never thought of success before. She had never had the opportunity to even try to be successful.

"I am willing to do whatever it takes," Abby said as she looked at Abe.

Abe looked over at John and put a hand on Abby's shoulder. "Well, John has something here he wants to share with you. Now it is only on loan, but we thought you might like to get started."

John walked to the back of the trailer, opened the door, unhooked the slant latch inside the horse trailer, untied the horse waiting inside, and led Piper out of the trailer.

He was a deep mahogany bay with four white socks and a blazed face. John looked at Abe, Abe nodded, then John handed the lead over to Abby. "He is yours to use while you stay here."

Abby stared at the big gelding standing in front of her for a moment. She was speechless. Her hands didn't move to reach for the lead. Her mouth was half open, but no words came out. She had handled a few horses and had helped out a little, but this was beyond her.

She blinked a couple of times, looked at Abe, then at Mr. Greenly with his extended hand holding the lead line of a beautiful horse.

"His name is Piper, and he is wanting some attention. Do you think that you can give it to him?" John asked quietly.

Abby almost panicked. "I don't know if I can." Reality was setting in. She had handled horses at Paige's and had been reading about them, but to have her own to take care of changed the whole concept; doubt was creeping in her mind. She leaned on her crutches a little to try to create an excuse.

"You can do anything you set your mind to," Abe stated. "You have saved a colt from a cougar attack, pulled him out of the mud. You can handle horses. You feed, water, so why not take the next step?"

Abby blinked a couple more times. She looked at Abe again to see if this was a dream. Abe nodded his head once as if giving permission to receive this gift. Then she lifted her hand away from her crutch, accepting the lead line. The horse attached to it stepped up to her. He dropped his head in front of her, and she reached up and stroked his head.

"I think it is a match, John," Abe said to lighten the mood a little.

"Go ahead and take him into the barn," Abe said as he and John closed the trailer door and began to talk.

"Just like that? You aren't going to help me lead him?"

"Nope I think you have him. If you can lead a mare with a little colt bucking around you, you can sure handle Piper and what he has to offer." Both men headed to the house.

Abby looked at Piper, then watched them leave. "I guess it is just you and me then," she said, a little uncertain as she stroked his head one more time. She moved her crutches and started to make her way to the barn, Piper following happily to a new place.

Patricia met both men on the porch with coffee. They sat and visited as Abby got acquainted with her newfound friend. She walked him to the barn and passed by the brush she used on Cricket the night before. She stopped him, picked it up, and began to brush him. He dropped his head as she began. There were tangles in his mane and mud on his hair. *It is going to take a little work to get him to look like Cricket,* she thought and she had plenty of time. Piper was happy to have a girl fuss over him again.

He licked his lips and resigned himself to the strokes of the brush.

By the second day of having Piper out at their house, Abe felt Abby was ready to take it to the next level. Abby had been out at the barn most of the morning. She had caught Piper and had brushed his hide until it had a polished shine to it. His mane and tail didn't have one tangle in them as she had brushed and braided, and brushed again to make sure. Piper's head was down and near asleep when Abe walked up behind her.

"Hey, Abbs, how is it going? Why don't we take him for a little ride?"

Abby turned and looked at Abe. "Really?"

"Bring him out to the round corral and I will grab his bridle," Abe said as he walked away.

Abby watched him walk toward the barn. She felt her heart in her throat. "Right now?"

"You ain't getting any younger," he said as he walked into the tack room.

"What saddle am I going to use?"

"You're not going to need a saddle right now. Just bring your horse and come on."

Abby untied Piper and started toward the round pen. Was he serious? Was he really going to let her ride?

She crutched her way to the gate with horse in tow. She seemed to limp a little more than she had a few minutes ago. Abe opened the gate for her as she led Piper in.

"Now what?" she asked as her heart starting thumping in her throat.

"Well, you said you wanted to learn to ride. And you have ridden horses before, so let's see what we can do with Piper."

"But where is the saddle? And what about my leg?"

Abe grinned at her. "You don't need a saddle and I think your leg is going to be just fine. Come here and let's take a look at what it is we need to do."

Abby walked up to Abe and handed him the lead line. Abe could see the fear penetrating Abby's body. Her whole posture was stiff and rigid.

"Why don't you step out of the round pen for a minute and let me warm him up for you. Alright?"

Abby seemed relieved. "Alright," she said as she crutched her way back to the gate, anxious to be out of the corral.

Abe turned Piper around a few times and with the lead line in one hand, he swung up on Piper's back.

Abby was shocked as Piper just stood there waiting for Abe to tell him what he wanted him to do.

Without hesitation, Abe asked him to move forward and Piper started off at a walk. Abe turned him both directions, stopped him and backed him up. Piper seemed happy to do what was requested. Abe stopped him and slipped off his back.

"Alright, Abbs, he is here for you."

Abby looked at him again, "Are you sure?"

"Well here is your chance to ride like I do. You said you wanted to ride more than anything…"

Abby swallowed hard. She opened the gate and walked back in.

"Now all we are going to do is get you on his back. Just listen to what I say and Piper will do the rest, alright?"

"Alright," Abby said, trying to gather her courage.

"First of all, I want you to put your hand on Piper's neck, close your eyes, take a deep breath, and ask, "How can I feel safe on this horse? Then let out your breath and do it again."

Abby looked at him for a moment like he was joking and he waited. She closed her eyes took a breath then asked herself, "How can I feel safe on this horse?" She let out her breath, opened her eyes, and looked at him, "Like that?"

"Ask again. Let your mind find the answer."

She closed her eyes again with her hand still sitting on Piper's neck, took a breath and asked, "How can I feel safe on this horse?" She took another breath and moved her hands back to his rib cage. She asked again without opening her eyes. She could feel him breathing. She moved her hands even more as she felt his sides extend out into a breath as she stated, "I can feel safe on this horse." She opened her eyes surprised at what she had said and looked at Abe.

"Are you ready?"

She nodded.

"Here we go. When you get on him, just breathe, relax, and ask yourself the same question. Trust Piper, trust me and trust yourself."

She nodded again and before she knew it, Abe lifted her as she swung her leg over Piper's back. She was on without a second thought.

"Breathe," Abe said as he saw her tense up, "and ask yourself."

Abby took a breath and asked again, "How can I feel safe on Piper?"

"Feel him breathe under you, loosen your legs, and just sit like you are sitting straddled on a chair and can't touch the ground. Grab his mane and let your legs dangle," Abe coached.

Abby took another breath and asked again. She released her legs a little and tried to pretend to be sitting on a chair backward. And sure enough, she began to feel him breathe under her. Piper stood with his head down and relaxed as Abe stroked his neck.

"As we start to move, Abby, you will feel him move underneath you. Let him take you with him, alright? Here we go." Piper took a few steps and Abe stopped him as she started to grip with her legs. "Here we go again," he coached as she settled in for the movement. By the third start and stop, Abby found the movement and moved with him as Abe led him around the round pen. "This is where it all begins, Abbs. You feel him and he feels you, this is where communication begins."

Abby looked at him and grinned. She was riding a horse, her leg didn't hurt, and she felt safe.

"So from here," Abe stated, "I want you to close your eyes when you feel safe and I want you to feel him move under you. Tell me when you feel his left hind leg leave the ground."

She looked at him confused.

"I will start you out then you follow from there, alright? Pay attention to how your body sways to the rhythm of his walking."

So as Abe led Piper around the pen, Abby started to trust and closed her eyes, feeling the sway of her body to the motion of Piper.

Abe stated, "Left, left, left." Every time Piper's left hind foot came up.

Abby found the rhythm and mimicked him. "Left, left, left." As they walked.

Feel it with your body, your legs, your hips, your back. His legs are your legs as you let him walk beneath you."

Abby smiled. She felt it. Then she lost the feel and missed the stride.

"Don't think," Abe coached, "feel."

She closed her eyes again and waited for her body to feel the left hind foot. "Don't think, feel." She repeated to herself. "Go with the motion."

"Excellent, you are a natural," Abe stated as he led her around again.

16

The day after Paige's incident, Craig loaded Libby in the stock trailer and headed to her house to feed and check on her horses. He pulled up in the driveway and unloaded Libby, leading her to the pasture. Libby seemed happy to be home. Guiding Craig to the gate, she waited for him to open it. He stopped for a moment before he undid the latch as he looked at the golden horse he held in his hand. Her eyes were kind, and she had a patience about her. "The stories you could tell," he said to her as he looked into her silent knowing eyes for a moment. He gently ran his hand down her neck, the sting welts still visible and tender to the touch. He led her back to the barn and found some bug spray in the tack room. There was no need in having anything else bite her today. He thought how several years prior he had led her to a stall at the fairgrounds when she was a three-year-old. That horse show seemed to be a changing factor in not only his life, but in so many people around him. He thought of how amazing an animal she was, gentle, strong, silent, and bold. Yet without someone to tell her story, that history would be hidden behind her eyes. He sprayed her down with bug spray, gave her a handful of grain, then led her back to the gate. He paused one more time then turned her out.

How odd it is to be standing here, he thought as he watched her walk away and join the other two horses in the pasture. Paige Cason, a girl he barely knew, yet someone he seemed to have known his whole life. So easy to be around so many years ago, and here he was at her doorstep taking care of her place for a couple of days.

He walked to the barn where Cougar and the broodmare stood in the stall. Cougar was anxious to be turned out. He bucked and played in the stall the best he could but preferred to have room to move about. Craig grabbed the halter and slipped it on the mare. He would turn them loose in the paddock they were in the previous day to let Cougar have his play before they headed home. The yellow colt bounced and played all the way to the paddock and raced around the fence line like he was on fire. Craig stepped outside the fence and watched Cougar. "What a cat you are," he said as he watched with admiration as the baby, ducked, dodged, and danced with his own shadow. The broodmare had her head down eating grass, seeming pleased to have her baby out where he could move.

Craig stood in the silence. How long had it been since he heard nothing? His ears searched for the busyness of the day, like at home…or New York, home didn't sound right to him, not there anyway. It seemed a lifetime away from where he was yesterday. A few birds were the only thing he heard, no barking dogs, no cars, or people bustling around. He turned and walked over to the haystack and got a forkful of hay for Libby and her cronies then checked their water. He walked back into the barn, grabbed the wheelbarrow, and manure fork and mucked out the broodmare's stall. He was taking her and Cougar home today, so he stripped it clean.

When Craig was done cleaning the stall and had put everything away, he walked around Paige's house and made sure everything was locked and in place. Then he went and loaded the broodmare and her yellow colt. He got in the pickup and paused before he pulled out. Tomorrow he would water her lawn and go get that load of hay for her. He would call Abe and Patricia later and let them know that he picked up the mare and colt and had checked on things here. He would spend the afternoon with Paige in the hospital and wanted to get a couple of posts set in the old corral at his dad's place. It seemed he had plenty to do while he was on vacation. He smiled as he put the truck in gear.

17

Paige had been released from the hospital. They had counted fifty-eight stings on her body, and she thought she could pinpoint each one of them. She was getting her strength back, not a hundred percent but getting better every day. For the last few days, she was spending more time outside on the front porch. Her feelings of having a hangover were now just a passing thought. She actually felt good enough to go out to the barn and spend a little time with the horses.

The mid-morning breeze felt good on her face as she opened the gate. She whistled for Libby, who came trotting over to see her. Paige put the halter on her to bring her in, give her a little grain, and see how she faired the wasps. Libby had recuperated faster than Paige had anticipated.

"Boy, little lady, I wish I could heal as fast as you did." She ran her hand down Libby's neck, across her withers and down her back. There was no sign of any stings. She reached down and scratched Libby's chest for a few minutes. Libby stretched out her neck and stuck out her upper lip, cocking her head to the side in the pure pleasure of an unreachable itchy spot.

Blue lay down inside the barn door just out of the sun, watching Paige. She had not left Paige's side since the incident.

Paige heard the phone ring, and Abby called from the deck of the house, "Paige, it is your mom."

"I will be right there," she said as she laid down the brush and left Libby to finish her grain. She walked past the hay that Craig had hauled in and stacked. She felt a lift in her heart for a moment. She couldn't believe that he was back here and had showed up out of nowhere. He had actually saved her life a week ago. It felt strange to think that life could be taken away so fast. Then he came in and sat with her at the hospital. She smiled to herself. That was the second time he had come to see her at a hospital, the second time he had come to her rescue. It was really good to see him. She breathed in the sweet smell of fresh hay as she walked by. It felt good to be alive. She jogged the rest of the way to the house and answered the phone.

"Hey, Mom, what's up?"

"Hey, Paige, your dad and I are going to a movie

and wanted to know if you and Abby were up for it this evening. It is supposed to be a comedy," Patricia said, her voice energetic.

Paige thought for a moment and turned to ask Abby, "Hey, Abbs, Mom and Dad are going to the movies tonight. Do you want to go with them?"

Abby was ecstatic. "Sure! What is playing?"

"Mom says it is a comedy, but I don't know the name of it. They will take you to dinner too," Paige teased.

"Are we going for Chinese?"

"I think that is where they are headed."

Paige grinned as she heard her mother on the other end. "Hey, babe, I think we are going out for Chinese tonight."

"Mom, Abby would like to go, but I think I am going to stay home tonight."

"Are you feeling alright?" Patricia asked a little concerned.

"Yeah, I am feeling pretty dang good actually. I am just feeling that home is a good place to be this evening."

"Alright, then we will drop by and pick Abby up about five thirty."

"She will be ready, I'm sure." Paige smiled.

"Do you want anything from town?"

"Nope, I think I am good, Mom."

"Well if you do, let me know and I will pick it up on my way through."

"Alright, I will."

"See you this evening then," Patricia said.

Paige hung up the phone and sat there for a moment. She heard Abby singing with the radio.

"I am heading back down to the barn."

"Alright," Abby said through her open bedroom door. "I am going to hang a few more horse pictures."

Paige smiled as she walked back down to the barn. Libby nickered softly as Paige approached. "You are like therapy, Libby." Paige sighed. She picked up her brush and began long strokes down Libby's golden neck.

***

At twenty after five, Abe and Patricia pulled into the driveway to pick up Abby. Patricia got out of the pickup, reached in the back, and pulled out an armful of rhubarb as Abe grabbed a flat of strawberries.

"Thought you might want to make some jam while you're hanging around the house," Patricia said with a smile.

"What? You're not going to make it for me?" Paige asked acting surprised.

"Nope, I have thirty pints at my house. It is your turn to make a few. Abby helped me, so she knows how to do it."

Abby looked at the armload Patricia was packing, "Oh really, more rhubarb?"

"Tis the season, Abbs, you will be happy in the winter when you want it."

"Actually making jam was kind of fun to do, I don't mind it at all."

"Well, now we know what we can do tomorrow," Paige piped in as she grabbed the flat of strawberries from her dad. Abe grinned.

"You know you could cancel the movies and we could make it tonight," Paige hinted, hoping for a little help.

"Nope we got a date with the Chinese restaurant. Can't cancel that, can we, Abby?" Abe said as he started heading back to the truck.

"I am so hungry for sweet and sour shrimp it ain't funny," Abby said. "The jam can wait!"

Paige put the flat of strawberries on the counter as her mom laid the rhubarb stems next to the sink.

"I have already washed and cleaned these, Paige. Do you want me to rinse them off?"

"No, Mom, I got it. You guys go ahead. This won't take any time to get them put away."

"Are you sure?" Patricia looked at her daughter, a little concerned, yet Paige looked so much better. Her color was back and her voice was strong. Patricia felt a little guilty for dropping off the rhubarb now. "If you need any help tomorrow, I can come back, Sis."

"Mom, I am fine, really. You guys go out and have a good time. Abby and I will play with this stuff tomorrow. We will have a taste test to see who makes the better jam." Paige grinned and raised an eyebrow as a challenge.

Abe grinned. "I will be the judge!" The girls looked at him. "On second thought, maybe I won't." He thought of having three women to deal with. "I think I will just eat it." He paused in a little awkward silence. "Well are we ready to go?" he asked as he started toward the door.

Abby grabbed her jacket. "See you later, Paige."

Paige walked them to the door. "Have a great time," she said as she watched them get into the Ford. Abe turned on the key, waved at her, then pulled out and headed down the driveway.

It was quiet. Paige was alone. She hadn't been alone

since the accident. She reached down and stroked Blue's head silently, then turned to go back in the house.

She rinsed the rhubarb again and chopped it, letting the knife cut through the freshness and pulling the strings from the stems getting ready for jam in the morning. The strawberries she put out on the porch. She heard a whir of wings and turned to watch two hummingbirds bicker over the feeder. She sat down on the porch listening to the drumbeat of tiny wings and watching them dance in the air. Effortless motion, speed, agility and strength were all woven together in a tiny bird body, and she watched in admiration as they floated around each other. Her stomach growled. Chinese food was beginning to sound pretty good.

Paige heard a rig coming up the gravel driveway, and Libby nickered in recognition. Paige looked over to see Craig pull up in his black jeep. He turned off the motor and grinned at her.

"Thought you might be hungry," he said with a grin. He grabbed a pizza out of the passenger side.

She smiled at him. "I could eat."

He had a boyish type attitude that made her feel like he might be up to no good.

Her suspicion got the best of her. "What? Did Mom put you up to this?"

"What? Where is Abby, I got her Canadian bacon with extra pineapple." He started looking around.

"She went to the movies with Mom and Dad tonight. I thought I would stay home and have some quiet time." Paige paused. "So Mom didn't call you to come and check on me?"

"I haven't talked to your mom in a couple of days," Craig said. "Should I be concerned?" He strode up on the porch and put the pizza down on the little patio table.

"No, not at all, I just thought for a moment that... Oh it is no big deal." The pizza smelled delicious, and her mouth began to water.

"You want some lemonade or a beer? I have both," she said as she got up from her chair. "I will get some plates and napkins."

"I would take a beer if you have one." He paused for a moment. "On second thought, just make that a lemonade," he said. "Let me help you."

He followed her into the kitchen. She grabbed two glasses and put a few ice cubes in each glass then grabbed the lemonade and filled them.

Craig grabbed the plates and napkins then both went back out onto the porch. Craig held the door for her. She looked so much better than a couple days before. They hadn't really talked while she was in the hospital, and it was good to have some quiet time with her now. He was pensive for a moment. "You look good. How are you feeling?"

"Much better. It took a few days to get my strength back but it seems to be coming back fast." She smiled at him.

"I couldn't believe it when I saw you and Libby running out of the timber," Craig began. "I thought I was going to see a herd of elk coming out into the open. I was really surprised to see that a single horse could make that much noise. It seemed like a dream." He thought for a moment, "I think I am going to give you an Indian name." He paused as if in thought.

Paige looked surprised, "Really?" Not knowing what to say.

"Yeah, something like um…" he thought again, "She Who Runs With Horses or maybe Running Horse or maybe just Stinging Bee.

Paige laughed. "Yeah," she thought for a moment. "Seems like every time I meet up with you, I am making some sort of grand entry." She rubbed the back of her head. "Looks like I am still working on my dismount."

Craig laughed.

Paige continued, "I guess I would call you Sir Saves A Lot."

"That isn't an Indian name." He laughed.

"Nope but is sure seems like you're my knight in shining armor." Paige grinned. "That is twice you have saved me—first at the fairgrounds and then the other day. What a strange day," Paige remembered. "I had no idea what was going on for a little while. I was just having a nice ride and was lost in thought when all of a sudden I heard wasps, lots and lots of them. Libby started to dance around, and I knew if she started bucking, I was not going to stay in the middle of her. I tried to get her to run, but she kept tucking her tail and trying to face her attackers."

"Boy you both were covered," he said then he was quiet again. "I have to apologize for taking off your clothes. I sure didn't know what to do, you had wasps everywhere, Paige." He felt like he had to explain. "But the important thing is that you are alright. I was pretty nervous for a while."

"Well I am sure glad you were there. What were you doing anyway? What brought you back home?"

He thought for a minute. *Home*, yeah, he was home. "Oh, it is a long story, and I don't want to bore you with details."

"I am all ears, I have nothing but time." She leaned forward and took a sip of her lemonade.

"Well in that case I think I will have that beer you offered," he said with a sigh. "Are you sure you want to hear this?"

She went in, got him a beer, and grabbed a glass of wine. It looked like it might be a long story.

She came out, put up her feet, grabbed a piece of pizza and said, "Alright, cowboy, tell me your story."

He smiled. "Well it goes something like this…" He paused, "Where do I begin? After graduation…"

Paige listened as he talked of his friends getting beaten up, self-defense classes, becoming a cop. Then he talked of his marriage and of the baby, of the plan to come back to Oregon so that his dad could meet his grandchild. He talked of the funeral and how nothing seemed to make sense. He spoke of just getting back on his feet and feeling pretty good, then of the family suicide. He talked of his partner reminding him of the tickets and of boarding the plane not three weeks later. Then coming home and finding her covered in wasps, he ended it there.

"They say things happen in threes and I am just praying that I am done."

Paige was quiet. She didn't know what to say. She took a sip of wine. It was the first sip that she had since the story began.

"You were going to be a dad?" She thought of that for a moment. "Wow."

He cut her off and broke her train of thought. "Now that is my story. What about you? Are you still drawing?"

"Yeah, I design barns and landscapes and that type of stuff. I haven't drawn just to draw for quite a while until just the other day." Paige hesitated. Should she show him the drawing of the horse, and what she thought about before she drew it? Or should she just keep it to herself?

"Is the drawing something you want me to see?" he asked, curious of her hesitation.

Paige looked at him surprised that he might be able to read her mind.

"Well I don't know. I haven't drawn for quite a while and I wasn't prepared to share it but…"

"Don't tell me you have it under the bed in a sketch pad," he said with a grin, remembering when they were teenagers at Paige's old place.

"No. It is not under my bed." Paige's face reddened with embarrassment. "I have it right here." She got up, went into the kitchen, picked up her sketchpad, and brought it out for him to see. She flipped through the pages until she came to the buckskin with the war bridle and feather. She handed it to him with a bit of defiance.

Craig took the book and looked at the drawing. Under it read, *From the Heart*. "Wow, Paige, this is incredible!"

Paige blushed.

"Have you done any shows or anything like that?"

"No. I haven't drawn in so long, Craig, I've been busy with other things. That one there just kind of jumped out of me the other day. Before I knew it, I had it down on paper."

"Paige this is beautiful."

"Thanks." She took another sip of wine and was quiet.

Craig paused and put down the book. He didn't want to put her on the spot about her drawings. "So is there anyone special in your life?" he pried, completely changing the subject.

"I have my family."

"I was thinking more on relationships."

"Oh," she paused. "No, never met anyone that really tickled my fancy, I guess," she answered.

"Really?" He pushed her a little harder to answer the question.

"I go out on dates once in a while," she snapped. "But just haven't found anyone who can put up with me."

"I see," he teased. "So what about me?"

"What about you?" she shot back.

"Would you be interested in going out with me?"

"I don't know…" she played back at him. "What do you have to offer me?"

"Well," he looked around playfully, "cold pizza, for starters." He shot her a look then asked, "What do you have to offer me?"

She was up to the challenge. "Well, you have already ridden my horse, so that won't do." She paused a moment. "So I guess I can only offer you a good sense of humor."

"Sold!" Craig laughed.

The crickets echoed back and forth as a yippy coyote attempted to sing out of tune searching for its mate. They both got quiet.

"Now what?" Craig said as they let the sunlight fade away.

"I don't know," Paige answered. Then out of the blue she asked, "Do you remember that kiss you gave me back at the old place?"

"Never forgot it," Craig said. "I think I would have done it differently had I known how much it meant to me."

"Hmmm, I remember it too." Paige sighed. "What do you mean done it differently?"

"I don't know," Craig answered. He had spoken before he thought things through and now his honesty had him in a pickle. He didn't want words to describe his thought and get it all messed up. He shook his head a couple of times, then took a breath and looked at her.

"Would you mind if I did it again?" he asked, a little more self-conscious. Then he grinned. "I mean if you are curious, I would just as soon show you than tell you."

She looked at him and paused. She hadn't talked to Craig in years, yet here he was sitting with her on the porch like he had never left. She had a connection with him unlike anybody she had been around. *That is silly*, she thought, but she felt it deep in her heart. She closed her eyes for a moment and sighed.

He couldn't believe he asked her for a kiss. What was he thinking? "Sorry, that was kind of silly," he laughed. "Didn't mean to put you on the spot, Paige. I don't know what I was thinking." He cleared his throat and slapped his leg to change the conversation.

Paige looked at him again as a calmness settled over her. "No, Craig, now you have me curious."

Craig paused and looked at her. "Really? I mean, are you sure?"

"I am sure." Paige smiled at him. "What would you have done differently?"

Without thought or hesitation and out of pure emotion, Craig silently stood up, stepped to her, took her hands and gently pulled her up to him.

He brushed her hair back and tucked it behind her ear, cupping her face in his hands and looking into her blue eyes.

He drew his face close to hers, anticipating a kiss. Paige became breathless. He took his hand behind her neck and drew her to him. He pressed his lips gently to hers, a soft warm kiss. He pulled away and looked at her again, still cupping her face in his hands.

Paige felt weak in the knees. She opened her eyes.

"I have got to go," he said in a whisper. "I really have to go." He lifted her hands to his lips and softly kissed them, then turned to go down the steps. He took two steps, missed the third, and fell on the lawn.

"Oh, Craig, are you alright?" She had to stifle a laugh.

"I'm good, I'm good," he repeated as he picked himself up off the ground, raising his hands up in the air like an Olympian who had mastered a landing. "Boy and they say don't drink and drive." He dusted himself off while heading toward his jeep. He looked back at her. "So, Paige, does that mean you will go out with me?"

He gave her a quirky little grin.

Not thinking, she answered, "Yeah, I probably would."

"How about tomorrow night?" He came back into the light of the porch.

She looked at him for some time. The glow of the evening was fading in her face as reality started sinking in. "Craig…" she paused. "I just don't know." She dropped her hands down to her sides. "You are getting ready to leave again." She looked unhappy. The mood was gone. The reality of him here, then the thought of him leaving. He was only here on borrowed time. She knew what she wanted but the ache that would follow grabbed her heart.

He came back and sat on the step. He didn't trust the porch now. "Paige, I get swallowed up in New York. I can't breathe there. I want to come back home. I'd put in for a transfer here, but I don't know if I want to be a cop anymore. I want to build things. I want to live and create. I know it sounds a little corny." He looked into her eyes again. "Paige, go out with me and let's see where that leads."

She had sat down next to him and looked him square in the eyes. "I don't know where my life is leading right now. With Abby and the horses and work, I can't seem to get it all done." She paused. "I am pretty tightly wound and a little complicated."

"All I am asking, Paige, is if you would go out with me? I want to share some time with you." He was serious. He took her hands into his. "I want to get to know you. How can I do that if you won't go out with me?"

She looked at him silently, then nodded her head. "Alright," she said. "I guess I get a little mellow dramatic with a kiss like that." She tussled his hair. She stood up, and he followed. He leaned forward for one more kiss, but she backed away. "Not tonight, cowboy. I don't want you to break your neck."

He stood quietly in front of her a moment. "Here," Craig whispered as he reached his hands up to her neck.

Paige froze in unexpected anticipation. Her heart was beating in her throat.

With a feather light touch, he gently took hold of the delicate crucifix cross of her necklace that was attached with a fine silver chain. He stood holding it a moment and quietly said, "Make a wish." He pulled the clasp of the fine chain, moving it back behind her neck. He laid the cross gently on her throat line.

Paige closed her eyes. She couldn't breathe. *Make a wish,* she thought, *my wish is standing in front of me.* She opened them.

He held her gaze for a moment, then stepped off the last step safely onto the lawn. He walked to his jeep, and this time he got in. "Tomorrow at six then. Dress casual, it will be a nature thing," he said as he started the engine.

She nodded in his headlights. He turned down the driveway. Restless Heart was singing on his radio, "The Bluest Eyes in Texas."

Wow, Paige thought as she picked up her half-empty glass of wine. She reached for his beer bottle. He hadn't taken a sip out of it. She smiled as she walked into the house.

18

The next morning, after feeding the horses, Abby talked about all that Abe and Patricia had done with her. The dinner, the movie, popcorn and an ice cream after the movie, all tumbled out in a jumble of sentences.

Paige had to smile. "Abby, I am so glad you got to go out with them. They are amazing people."

"I know," she said as she filled her cereal bowl with Lucky Charms and poured in the milk.

"We will get the strawberries out and get them cleaned up. I cut up the rhubarb last night." Paige put the rhubarb in the pan. "Let's see, we need six cups of sugar for two and a half pounds of rhubarb and one and half pounds of strawberries as well as orange juice and pectin." Paige added , orange juice, and sugar, and turned it on medium.

"I will grab the jars after I eat breakfast," Abby said, confident in the routine of making the jam at Patricia's place as she shoved a spoonful of cereal into her mouth.

"I think I will have a bowl too," Paige said as she grabbed a bowl out of the cupboard.

"How would you like to go and spend the night out at Mom and Dad's?" Paige asked as she chopped up a strawberry for the top of her cereal.

"What are you going to do?" Abby asked.

"Well, Craig wants to take me out tonight, and I don't want you sitting at home by yourself." Paige felt herself blush and hoped Abby wouldn't notice.

"Can Blue come with me?" she asked hopefully. The dog seemed to be a security blanket.

"Sure, if she wants to. She enjoys it out there," Paige answered.

Abby beamed. She was anxious to ride Piper again. With that thought she piped up. "Did I tell you that I loped Piper the other day?"

"That is what I hear. Dad said that you are a natural. Piper has quite a story behind him. You will have to hear it someday."

"Abe said it is your friend's horse, John Greenly's daughter."

Paige smiled, "Yes, her name is Samantha, and we have a little history too. She just had a baby. I have got to go see her sometime. I haven't seen her since he was born. Maybe I will take you out there so you can meet her. We will call Mom a little later and make sure that you can stay."

As the rhubarb started heating up, Abby asked, "Paige, do you mind if I give Blue a bath?"

"I suppose you can, if you can get her in the tub." Paige smiled.

Blue tucked her docked tail and slinked under the table at hearing her name and the word "bath" in the same sentence. She knew it couldn't be a good thing.

How do they know? Paige wondered.

Abby finished her cereal and crutched her way to the pantry for a case of pint jars. While she was there, she grabbed a dog bone snack for Blue, thinking it might help with the bath thing.

Abby called to her. "Blue, here you go, girl. Here is a snack."

Blue looked at her cautiously, dropped her head, and took the treat. Abby snapped the leash on her collar. "We are going to give you a bath, girl, and you are going to be the prettiest dog in town."

Blue tried to turn and go back under the table, but the leash pulled tight. Blue sat down, looking at Paige.

"Don't look at me." Paige laughed at the sad look on her dog's face and said defensively, "It wasn't my idea."

Abby pulled on the leash, but Blue laid down. "Come on, Blue. Come on, girl."

Blue was sullen and wouldn't budge.

"Why don't you go start the water in the tub? I don't think she is going anywhere right now."

Abby looked at the mournful look on Blue's face. "She doesn't like baths much, does she?"

"Not really," Paige replied with a grin.

Paige finished her cereal, got up from the table, and washed her bowl. Then she turned her attention to the rhubarb on the stove.

With a small tug of war, Abby got Blue into the bathroom. Getting her in the bathroom and getting her into the bathtub were two totally different wars. Paige knew it was going to be a battle of the minds. She quietly listened to the thumping around in the other room and smiled at the attempts of a strong-willed girl and a bull-headed dog.

"Come on, Blue… No you don't…" A grunt. "Put your feet right there. No, Blue. Come on, you can do it." Then there was a splash.

With a smile, Paige had to wonder whether it was Abby in the tub or the dog. Blue could think of every conceivable way of keeping her feet from getting in that tub. Paige had to still herself from looking.

"Good girl." Was heard so Paige knew no one was drowning and figured the girl had won the battle.

"Don't forget, you are going to clean up the mess after you're done," Paige warned.

"I will." Came the reply from through the wall.

Ten minutes later, a disheveled dog looking more like a dripping drowned rat came sailing down the hallway followed by a soaked happy girl packing a towel.

"Take her outside before she…" Paige didn't have time to finish her sentence.

Blue, with her dripping self, gave a tremendous all-body shake, spraying water like a sprinkler all over the front room. Then she took off across the carpet, flopped down like a fish out of water and started rubbing herself on the floor.

"Grab her, Abbs! Get her outside so she can do that out on the grass."

Abby went to grab Blue, but before she made it half way across the room, Blue took off across the front room and down the hallway. Blue dove past her, ran into Abby's room, and jumped on her bed, rolling her wet dripping body all over Abby's bed and saturating not only her blankets and sheets but her pillow too.

"No, Blue!" Abby hollered as she hobbled to the bedroom door.

Blue sailed off the bed and ran between Abby and the door. She headed back out to the front room.

Paige opened the kitchen door and called to her. Blue flew out the door and around the yard.

Abby crutched her way back into the kitchen to see what had happened to her dog. There were wet dog prints everywhere.

Paige was stirring her rhubarb with a grin on her face. "Next time you might want to put a leash on her before you get her out of the tub."

"I didn't think she would do that. You said she didn't like baths."

"She doesn't, but I didn't say anything about after the bath." Paige smiled. "You said something about cleaning up the mess…"

"I know," Abby replied with a glance at the wet kitchen floor and hallway. Then she realized that in less than a minute, Blue had dripped water through the entire house. "She even got my bed wet!"

"I know." Paige smiled. "So much for helping me with the jam this morning."

"Yeah, well so much for me making my bed this morning," Abbie stated as she headed back to her bedroom and began to pull her sheets off her bed.

Paige shook her head while grinning. She finished filling another jar, wiped the rim with her towel, tightening the lid snugly and turning it upside down on a towel with the other freshly filled jars.

After cleaning up Blue's mess, cleaning the bathroom, mopping the kitchen, changing the sheets and blankets on her bed, vacuuming, and even having to wipe down and dust the pictures on the wall that had water marks from the rogue water sprinkler, Abby wondered if she would ever give another dog a bath.

She sat down at the table as Paige poured beautiful strawberry rhubarb jam into another pint jar. "Did you and your mom do this a lot?"

"Do what a lot?" Paige asked as she moved the jar on to a towel with the other pints.

"Make stuff and can food."

"Sure, back then we didn't really have a choice. But now I just like knowing that I can reach in the cupboard and grab something that we have made. It is kind of refreshing."

"I didn't do anything like that with my mom. Every Saturday we would go down to the market and buy our groceries. She would sit and make a menu of what we were going to eat for the week, then we would go buy it." Abby thought for a moment. "We had a little freezer on the bottom of the refrigerator. Nothing like what you have." She looked at the chest freezer in the washroom and the pantry full of canned food and dried goods.

As Paige listened, she realized this was the first time that Abby really spoke of her mother and her old life. It had to be a culture shock to live miles from nowhere when the market could be just down the street.

"I bet your mom was amazing."

"She was. I can still hear her voice sometimes. She was real careful and always overprotective of me. Sometimes it would drive me crazy."

Paige thought for a moment of what it would be like without her mom or her dad. She couldn't fathom it.

"Well I guess that is where we come in. You have time to learn how to can and cook with us. Mom loves to work in the kitchen and share her knowledge. But first," Paige looked outside at the dog still rolling in the grass. "I think you better go out and catch Blue and get her brushed out. If not, she is going to be a mess. Her brush is in the mud room on the top shelf."

"I love working in the kitchen with your mom. She is a lot of fun." Abby crutched into the mud room reaching above the washer for the brush. She then headed out to the yard, calling to Blue.

Blue paraded around with a red scarf around her neck and her coat brushed to a silky blue sheen. She acted like she was the prettiest dog in the country. Abby then packed her sleeping bag, pillow, her pajamas and a set of clothes preparing for a day with horses and gardening.

Just as they were getting ready to leave out to Haines to spend the afternoon with Paige's parents and have lunch, Abby said, "Wait." She ran back into the house and grabbed a jar of freshly made jam. She glanced at Paige with a sheepish grin. "In case Abe wants to be a judge."

Paige laughed, "Get in the truck," she said as she patted Abby on the shoulder.

When they arrived, Abby proceeded to tell Abe and Patricia the story of the bath and trying to decide who got wetter, Blue or herself. "And I have learned to put the leash back on her after I am done washing and not to let her jump out of the tub expecting her to just stand there to be towel dried." Abby continued, "She went through the house like a bullet, and in less than one minute had almost every room soaked, including my bed—and I had to clean it up!"

"I thought maybe she didn't want to do anymore jam and wanted to do housework instead," Paige piped in.

"I think the jam would have been easier."

"Yeah but now I have a clean house and jam in the cupboard." Paige was grinning. "We killed two birds with one stone."

"I even brought you a pint if you wanted to judge it, Abe," Abby stated with a grin.

"Uh, I think I will just enjoy it without judgment," Abe said, looking over at Patricia and winking.

Everyone laughed as they finished lunch.

Abby went to the barn, grabbed her halter and headed out to catch Piper after lunch. She wanted to show Paige how much she had learned since she had been out there. Horses seemed to be like a mystery novel with adventure, trust, and courage all wrapped up in an unspoken language. And once you started learning it, it was addictive as candy on the tongue.

Paige watched her with pride. Abby was glowing with life and vitality. She didn't even look like the same girl who was hobbling from the bedroom to the front room couch, locking herself in the house for hours on end. All of that was gone. This girl was catching Piper by herself and leading him into the barn, brush in one hand and horse in the other. She was becoming a confident young lady.

The afternoon went quickly for Paige. She watched Abby proudly ride Piper, taking him through his paces of walk, trot, and canter in the round pen and practicing opening the gate. Paige listened as her dad instructed Abbey to lift her leg, relax, or breathe. It brought back so many memories of him working with Paige. She smiled with pride and admiration of her father.

***

When Paige got home it was just after five. She went to the barn and checked the horses, ran new water in the trough, and closed the corral gate. She jumped in the shower and let the cool water run over her body. She closed her eyes, and for a moment everything was quiet. The house almost felt empty without Abby there. It felt good to let the water wash away all the day's dirt and leave her feeling refreshed. Paige towel dried her hair and then slipped on a newer blouse and pants. She slipped on a pair of flat sandals and buckled them at the ankle. Then she brushed back her sandy blonde hair and braided it into a half-French braid.

At six o'clock Paige heard the familiar sound of Craig's jeep pull in front of the house. He turned off the engine and walked to the gate as she came out the door. He said, "Hey, Paige, grab your swimming suit if you don't want to skinny dip." His eyes twinkled.

"Where are we going?" she asked.

He looked at her and said, "No Tell'em Ridge."

She got a look of concern on her face, but then cut loose and said, "You know what, surprise me." She went back in to get her swimsuit and towels, and as an afterthought, went back and grabbed a sweatshirt.

Craig walked over to the corral while waiting and looked at Libby with her white mane flowing in the breeze. She nickered softly as she casually walked over to meet him at the fence. He stroked her blazed face and straightened her long white forelock to the center of her forehead. There was a peace about her as she closed her eyes and sighed.

"You are quite a mare, Libby," he said under his breath.

He thought of the day he raced her to his dad's place—the power, the grace of doing what he asked of her without hesitation—she was willing without question or judgment. There was no sign that day ever existed now. It was just a memory that he thought of, a moment in time between two beings never to be spoken of. He massaged her cheek a little as Libby dropped her head.

Paige walked out the door and saw the two standing there. *He is so gentle with her*, Paige thought. *Libby really likes him*. Paige had her little bag with swimsuit and towels and walked up to where they were standing.

"She is a nice mare, Paige," Craig said as he scratched just under the jaw line.

"I sure love her," she answered. "We have been down some roads her and me."

"I would love to hear the things you have done with her," he stated as he turned to look at Paige. Libby reached her nose out and nibbled on Paige's shirt.

"Well I guess I will have to tell you sometime."

They turned and walked back to the jeep. Libby watched them walk away, her head casually over the top rail of the fence.

They crawled in and headed down the driveway. As Craig turned on the paved road, Paige leaned back and let the wind blow in her face. She closed her eyes for a moment, just letting time blow by. She felt like a schoolgirl without a care in the world. She opened her eyes to see Craig smiling at her.

"Are you glad you are here?" he asked. With the grin that was on her face, he already knew the answer.

"I don't know yet." She smiled back.

"What do you mean, you don't know?"

"I don't know where here is yet, but I am sure enjoying the ride." She closed her eyes again as they started driving in the timber. The shadows of the trees and sun flickered like a strobe light behind her closed eyes. She opened them again and looked at Craig. He was driving with one hand on the steering wheel and the other on the stick shift. His sunglasses reflected the scenery as he drove. Everything seemed right. She had anticipated first date jitters or nervousness on what to say, but with Craig, there seemed to be an ease about him.

"What are you thinking?" she asked as she turned back to glance at the road for a moment.

Craig turned off the smooth dirt road and headed up a bumpier logging road, one not used much. "I am thinking…" He shifted down. "This just feels right." He looked at Paige and smiled. "What do you think?" He continued to look at her, not noticing the large rocks that had rolled off the upper bank into the middle of the old logging road.

"I think you should keep your eyes on the road," she cautioned as she grabbed for the roll bar.

Craig glanced at the road and just in time, gave a quick jerk on the wheel to barely miss a large rock.

Paige smiled. "Is this how you drive in New York?"

"Yep, and that was a pedestrian," Craig answered. He slowed down a little as he came to a tree that had fallen across the road and was wedged into a fork of another tree that was about eight feet off the ground. "And this is a semi-truck." He laughed. "Had to learn to dodge and duck." He glanced at Paige again.

"I see," she said. She felt herself duck her head as Craig drove under the fallen tree.

"Almost there," he said as he turned another corner coming out into a clearing. He drove until it leveled out into a wide-open spot, and there he parked the jeep and turned off the engine. They sat for a moment, the silence almost deafening. He leaned forward, draped both hands on the wheel, and looked at her with a grin. "We will walk from here." He grabbed a couple of blankets, pillows, and a basket filled with food out of the back. Paige helped, grabbing a bag with handles. It contained paper plates, utensils, napkins, a bottle of wine, and glasses.

"Where are we going?" she sounded excited.

He tucked the blankets and pillows under his basket arm and took her hand. "I will show you." He walked about fifty yards, and tucked in a little draw was a small creek that fed into a pool of water.

"This is where I used to come when I was a kid with my dad," he said. "Not many people know it is here."

"Did your mom ever come up here?"

"No, she didn't get into the nature thing. She is more a swimming pool, hot tub, spa kind of woman."

"I kind of like creeks myself," Paige stated. "Although it has been years since I swam in one."

"I remember this to be bigger when I was a kid." Craig paused. "But then, I think that is what happens as we grow up. Things are brought up to scale. Kind of like my dad. When I was a kid, he was huge. It seemed like no man was bigger. Now I am looking him in the eye."

Paige looked at him for a moment. "Oh your dad is big alright. It is just that you grew up to match him."

He set down the basket and shook out a blanket. Paige caught an end of it and squared her side, removing a few rocks. Craig grabbed a pillow and tossed it to her. She caught it fluffed it a little then set it on the edge of the blanket.

Craig fluffed the other and tossed it on the edge too.

"First I want to go swimming," he said. "Then we eat!" He walked up to the water and slipped off his shoes and his jeans. He had his swim trunks on underneath. Then he peeled off his shirt. He tested the water with his toes. "Brrrr," he said as he shivered.

His lean body made Paige look twice. She noticed he was not the long lanky thoroughbred she remembered him to be back when they were teenagers. Yet it was the same Craig who had, so many years ago, come into the hospital and checked on her after her accident at the fairgrounds. He was also the same Craig who apologized for taking off her clothes when she was attacked by the wasps.

"Hey, that's not fair. You knew where we were going. I have to change." Paige looked around for a tree or something to get behind. There was a little juniper to her right, so she slid behind it and changed as fast as she could.

She heard Craig jump in. "Wooo! Come on in. The water is fine," he said as he splashed around. He lay on his back and floated a little while until he saw her come down to the edge of the water.

Paige was beautiful in her one-piece swimsuit. She tested the water then waded in. Not one to prolong the agony of cool water, she dove in to get the shock over with. It was not a big pool but it was big enough to have a water fight in, and she was the first to instigate it. Craig obliged and shot water back at her. Paige hadn't swum in years, yet it was just like riding a bike. It came back to her fast. Soon she was floating on her back and just enjoying the evening sun, the fresh water, and good company.

"Are you glad you came?" Craig asked as he swam up next to her.

"I am," she said as she did a backstroke to stay afloat.

"Me too," he said as he dove under the water.

Paige noticed a tattoo on his shoulder as he came up for air. "What does that tattoo stand for?"

He looked over at his shoulder and the navigational star with an N on the top. "Oh I…" he hesitated. "I was searching for my North, hoping some day I would find it. I guess every tattoo has a story." He felt silly for speaking it out loud to her.

"I think it is pretty… cool." She paused, "I would say pretty but I don't think that was your intention when you got it." Paige grinned at her own humor as she lay back in the water." I always wondered about tattoos. I had thought of getting one but … I don't know, can't think of one I would want on my body the rest of my life, so I guess I will keep thinking." She smiled.

"Yeah, don't get one if you don't have a commitment to it," Craig stated. "I have heard some people get half way through it and decide they don't like it. That would be a nightmare." He started wading out. "I like mine. It is a reminder for me to keep moving forward. And just so you know, I think it is pretty too." He smiled. "I am going to get out, so I can set up dinner. You stay as long as you like."

"No I will get out and help you."

"No you won't," he remarked. "You stay right where you are." Craig grinned at her. "I got this."

Paige watched him get out of the water and walk over to where his shirt and jeans were. She noticed how lean he was. He had a few scars on his back and she wondered what they were from. She looked at the tattoo again. He slipped on his shirt.

She leaned back in the water and let herself float as she felt a little guilty letting someone wait on her. She kicked her legs a little and lost herself in relaxation. About ten more minutes and she was getting out of the water. The sun was warm and the feeling of being free seemed to fill the air. She couldn't remember the last time she had just relaxed, to just enjoy the moment and be.

She wrapped a towel around her middle and put her sandals on. She then draped her blouse over her shoulder as she came to see what Craig was up to.

He had opened the basket and laid out grapes and strawberries along with cantaloupe. Then he laid out crackers, meats and cheese, and a bottle of wine. It was the same wine she had last night at her house. He grabbed a strawberry and fed it to her as she walked by.

"Mmm, these are good," she said. She hadn't realized how hungry she was. "Ah, I see you pay attention to detail," she chided him as she looked at the wine.

"Yes, ma'am. I do on certain things," he added. "Sometimes some things go completely unnoticed, but for you, I will do my best."

She sat down on the blanket and slipped off her sandals. "This is really nice, Craig. I am so glad you brought me up here."

"I love it. I came up here the other day and knew I wanted to share it with you. I am really glad you like it." He sat across from her and asked, "Are you ready to eat?"

"I am," she said eagerly as he handed her a little plate.

"Can I get you some wine or would you like lemonade?" he asked in a professional server's tone.

"Oh, wine please," she teased back as she slipped on her sweatshirt.

They sat and ate as the first stars started peeking out into the darkening sky. Conversation was easy and casual.

Craig mentioned what he had read in the paper and who had died. He spoke of Samantha Greenly getting married and now having a kid. He lit a propane lantern and hung it on a tree limb to shed some light in the darkness but not take from the vast array of stars as they started peeking their way into the twilight. The North Star was the first to show itself.

"Is this hard for you, Craig?" Paige asked concerned. "I mean your baby and your wife?" She was unsure how to ask the question.

Craig looked at her and took a breath, thinking of how to answer it. "Death brings a finality, a feeling of immeasurable emptiness," he said. "But no matter how much I want to turn back the clock or change things, I can't. There will always be a special place in my heart for what I had with Lisa and the baby, and I wonder sometimes of the things I could have done differently." He sighed. "The one thing I learned is I can't go back and I am okay with that now." Craig bit into a strawberry. "Right now I can enjoy a few things that are here in front of me, in this moment. I try to live life with no regrets; I try not to take things for granted." He sighed as if to change the subject. "I think that Sam is going to be a great mom."

Paige listened with an open heart to what Craig had endured—to have loved and lost and found the strength to keep moving forward. Then she thought of Sam getting married and herself being one of the bridesmaids. *That was a good day*. "Yeah, I think she will be too."

"Have you ever thought of getting married?" Craig asked casually.

Paige thought about it for a minute then leaned back on the blanket. "Oh I don't know, I just haven't found anyone I really want to spend time with, I guess. I mean I like company and all of that, but I just don't feel connected to anyone around here." She rambled, "I mean I have a pretty busy lifestyle and I have a hard time keeping up with work, horses, and now Abby." Her voice trailed off. She basically repeated what she had said the night before, hoping that story would work.

"Actually," she paused, "I had fallen for a guy a long time ago."

"What happened to him?"

"He moved, got married, and started a family, last I heard." Paige paused, "I don't even know if he knew how I felt. Sometimes I guess you just have to let go."

"If he did, he was an idiot." Craig shot back, then lay back on the blanket. Wondering if it was him but not asking.

They both lay silently, listening to the evening come

alive. Craig marveled at how fast the darkness seemed to silently present itself…and looked up. The Milky Way was so vivid; it looked like dust among stars. "You can't see the stars where I live," he said dreamily.

"Really?" Paige sounded surprised.

"Well, you can, but not like this," he said and he spread his hand across the empty space in front of him.

They both lay there looking up. A shooting star sailed across the sky so fast then disappeared in the vastness of the night. They both gasped at the same time but neither could get the words out fast enough.

"To be honest with you, Craig," Paige said almost dreamily, "I haven't looked up at the stars in a long time. I used to do it a lot with Mom. I have forgotten how beautiful they are." She noticed the fingernail of the moon watching over the collection in the Milky Way.

"Stars are so amazing," he said. "They sit up there silent every night, patiently waiting to be seen, waiting for someone to look up to see the beauty and maybe question the mystery of the universe."

There was silence for a moment, nothing but Mother Nature's choir chirping their throaty song.

"Oh look, there is Orion," Paige said, surprised that she recognized it. She pointed to the bright ball of light in a small cluster of stars.

Craig looked where she was pointing and smiled, "And there are the Seven Sisters," he said, looking a few degrees to the south.

"Do you know the constellations?" she asked.

"Not all of them, but I know a few. They always fascinated me."

"Do you know of any other living being on the earth that looks at the stars and stares at them in wonder?"

"I hadn't thought of that, but no, none that I can think of," he replied. Then he paused, "It makes me wonder, how many millions of years have they seen? How many lifetimes they have witnessed?"

Paige looked again at the millions of tiny lights and stardust. She began to recite a poem.

"Many a night from yonder ivied casement, err I went to rest,
Did I look on great Orion, sloping slowly to the West.
Many a night I saw the Pleiades, rising thro' the mellow shade
Glitter like a swarm of fireflies tangled in a silent braid.
Here about the beach I wandered, nourishing a youth sublime
With the fairy tales of science and the long results of Time."

"You learned that in your freshman year," Craig said.

"Yeah, I always thought it sounded wonderful. It is a small bit out of *Locksley Hall* by Alfred Tennyson. I can't remember the whole poem, but I do remember it being about forbidden love and beauty and sadness and life. I love the way he put words together. I used to look at the stars so often. They just bring his words to life." Paige laughed as she repeated the name in a Lordly manner. "Lord... Alfred... Tennyson..."

Craig laughed with her.

"Do you believe in destiny, Paige?" he asked with a sigh, lying on his back cradling his head with his hands.

"Well I think things happen for a reason," she answered. "Why?" She was curious about what he was thinking.

"That is what I mean, I guess." He felt kind of foolish asking. He noticed he would never have talked to Lisa like this. Yet he felt like he could talk about anything with Paige. "I mean," he continued, "what are the odds of me seeing you and Libby the day of the wasps? Does it seem crazy to you or anything?"

Paige shrugged. "I hope it's not crazy, I think of the same things." She paused to consider, "I don't know why I went for a ride that day. We were getting ready to go get hay before the day got hot. The next thing I knew I had an urge to ride Libby that was beyond common sense. When I whistled to her, she came trotting down to see me. I just jumped on and rode." Paige thought for a moment.

"And why after months of isolation, did Abby decide to walk down to the spring that day and find Cougar?" Paige questioned the history of coincidences. She looked back up at the stars and stared. "Or," Paige paused again, "why did you come back here?"

"This is where I belong," Craig answered without hesitation. "I don't think I ever really let go of Oregon. This is my home."

"Is it?" Paige was quiet for a second. "Do we really ever let go?" she asked.

"No, I don't think so," he responded. "Not of things you truly love. You might get along alright, but there seems to be an emptiness or hole. Letting it go out of respect or necessity, trying in vain to fill the void, but always having that hollow feeling." Craig was silent for a moment as he let honesty consume him. "Yes, I think this is home, I can't imagine any other place I want to be, or anyone else that I want to share it with," Craig said as the truth penetrated in his heart. "I haven't felt this complete in years, Paige." New York seemed a lifetime away for Craig, a life that he didn't want to return to.

She propped herself on her elbow and looked at him, his familiar face shadowed by darkness and the knowledge in his words. She knew what he was talking about, though maybe not to the degree of loss in his life. She had felt the pain, the emptiness and the attempt of letting go, yet she also felt like somehow through the hurt and aloneness, certain things found their way back, if it was meant to be.

This moment right now could be lost forever. She wanted to hold onto it for a life time. "I have a question to ask you." She paused, her heart in her throat. "Would you kiss me again?"

Craig leaned up on his elbow and looked directly at her, speechless at the opportunity. He had wanted to kiss her ever since she walked out of her house that evening and every moment after. Now in this setting and in this mood, he had to be honest. "Paige, if I kissed you now," he paused, "I don't know if I could stop at just a kiss."

She was silent for moment, knowing that tomorrow would be another day with no promises made. Distance was going to separate them again. But this memory would last a lifetime, whatever the future may hold.

"What if I didn't want you to stop," she whispered. She looked at him intently for a moment, took a breath and closed her eyes. She repeated. "What if I didn't want you to stop?" She looked down at the blanket, maybe in fear of losing this moment and knowing he was going to leave, anticipating the pain to follow. But she pushed all that aside. Him being here and this evening was her wish.

He reached up and moved her hair from around her face, pushing it behind her shoulder. He lifted her chin and looked at her. "There is something about you that takes my breath away." He tried thinking of self-control. "Are you sure?" He paused for a sign of hesitation or second thoughts. His breath was hot against her skin.

"I have never been more certain about anything, Craig." She looked at him again and brought her hand up to touch his cheek. "You are beautiful." She drew her fingers down his jaw line. She ran them down along his neck, crossed his chest and rested her hand on his heart. She could feel it beating. She brought it back up behind his head running her fingers through his hair. Her hands were trembling. She leaned over and gently pressed her lips to his neck.

He caught his breath. He kissed her chin, then brought his lips alongside her neck just below her ear. He paused there. With effort, he pulled away and looked at her again. "Are you ok with this?" he asked.

Paige nodded. No words came out.

He gently touched his half-parted lips to hers, and she responded. He lost himself in the moment.

Paige melted into his arms.

Slow down, he thought. *Be with her in this moment, tomorrow doesn't exist.*

19

Paige stirred. She could hear the phone ringing but was not awake enough to answer it. She looked at the clock, nine thirty. Her body felt heavy, exhilarated, yet tired all at once. The answering machine picked it up. The words she heard made her sit straight up in bed.

"Hello, Paige, this is Ben from the Department of Human Services, and we are happy to inform you that we have found a permanent foster facility for Abigail Sorenson. We will be expecting to see you both on Tuesday at nine thirty a.m. Please bring all of her belongings and anything you want her to have. If you have any questions please feel free to call me. Thank you."

Paige felt sick. How could that happen? She got out of bed and walked to the phone. She picked it up, then put it back down. She paced for a few moments as she thought. For months she had expected to send Abby to another foster home. That was what was expected—a favor for a friend of a friend of a friend. She bit her bottom lip while she thought. She had thought she wanted her old life back, but what was her life without Abby? A strong-willed, bull-headed girl, who was only a child trying to get by. Oh God, she hadn't taken Abby to therapy, but that wouldn't make them find her a new foster home, would it? Paige needed to get her thoughts all lined out. She needed to talk to someone.

She picked up the phone again, knowing who she was going to call—someone, who might be able to give her some advice. But first she needed more information. She dialed the number from the answering machine.

"Department of Human Services, Ben," he answered.

"Hey, Ben, this is Paige Cason. I have Abby, I mean Abigail Sorenson. She is a foster child."

"Hello, Paige. Yes, isn't that great news? We have a permanent foster home for her, so she can get all the help she needs," he stated proudly. "We appreciate your help holding her as long as you have. After our last interview and her history, we thought we should put her in a special program. It is a school set up for troubled teens. She will be able to stay there until she is eighteen and will take classes to get her diploma and other classes that can help her with her loss and anger management. There are five therapists on campus at all times." Ben's whiney nasally voice reminded Paige of fingernails running down a chalkboard. "See, I told you we would get her out of your hair."

Paige was at a loss of what to say but made an attempt. "I don't think she needs to go to that school."

"What do you mean, Paige? You came by here weeks ago and said you wanted your life back. She was withdrawn and didn't know how to communicate. You talked as if she was almost suicidal." "I know," she said, "but things have changed. She has changed and I have changed. She has started to open up and become family."

"Well, that is good, so you have made progress with her. I will put that in my file. You know what you are feeling now is a panic of losing something. A lot of new temps go through it. It is kind of like finding a puppy and the original owners coming to claim it. You think you want to keep her, but she belongs to the state."

"She is not a puppy!" Paige blurted out. "She is a little girl who has lost her parents and is now finding her feet."

"Well, as I look in your file, Paige, you have not contacted us or brought her to therapy like we had scheduled. The last information I have in here is that you were only a temporary foster and you wanted your life back. The child was rude and didn't follow rules and was completely withdrawn."

"Yeah, but that was then. She has changed so much. I have changed." Paige sounded exhausted. "I am sorry that I did not bring her in for her therapy, but I didn't think she needed it."

"And who gave you the authority to make that decision? Do you have a degree as a doctor or a therapist? We have people who are specialists. It is our job to look out for the welfare of this child and make sure that she is socially acceptable to society. You think just because you have had her for a couple of months that you know what is best for her."

"Yes, I do."

"Two weeks ago you sounded lost and irritated. Now this week you are convinced you know what is best," Ben whined in defiance. "What will it be next week, Paige? You can't just change your mind when you want and have us come running in to save you. You asked for the removal of a foster child, and now I am answering your request."

"But if you could see her," Paige said, but it sounded like she had no grounds to stand on. Ben was on the phone to make a statement, not to listen or understand. He was there to take control of a situation as she had requested a few weeks prior.

He continued, "Just because you have one foster child does not make you an expert, Paige. I have seen hundreds of cases. It is my job to use my discretion and place these kids in places that are safe. From what I see in this folder, I feel that she would be better off in this special facility. She will be placed in a safe environment and monitored on her progress."

"But, Ben, I think…" Paige started.

Ben cut her off in mid-sentence. "Many children have a tendency to pretend that they are better just because they don't want to go back in the system. They want to stay where they are familiar. It is my experience that this program I am putting her in will be best for her erratic behavior and anger issues. She fits the criteria." He took a breath like he was reading out of a manual. "I do fully expect you to have Abigail Sorenson here on Tuesday at nine thirty a.m." He paused again to make the statement clear. "I have an appointment on another case, so I am going to have to go. Have a good day, Paige. Goodbye."

Paige hung up the phone. "I will show you criteria," she spat. She picked up the phone again. "You want anger management? I will show you anger management." She dialed Samantha Watterson's number.

Samantha and Paige's history went back to high school. At a horse show when Paige showed Libby for the first time. Samantha had given Paige a bad time at the show. That was the first time Paige had actually met Craig. Samantha had been pestering her all day when Paige had finally put her foot down and let Samantha know where she stood. After the horse show, John Greenly came to talk to Paige about her filly, Libby, and wanted to buy her.

While they were talking, a loud pop from an exploding balloon caught their attention and Samantha was being dragged by her horse, Piper. Paige, without thinking, jumped on Libby's bare back and ran to the rescue, catching the horse and saving the girl. There had been an article in the newspaper about it. After months of physical therapy and Abe working with Piper, Paige and Samantha had come to realize they weren't all that different. They became good friends.

And now Samantha's old horse, Piper, was the one Abby was learning to ride.

Sam was now married to Michael Watterson, attorney at law, for over three years, and had a son just a week old. Jonathon Harley what a cute name. Paige had not had time to see him.

The phone rang. Samantha answered, "Hello."

"Hey, Sam, it is Paige."

"Paige, how are you?" Sam said in a chipper voice.

"I am doing pretty good. How is motherhood treating you?"

"Pretty well, I sure can't complain much. Michael's family is here to help me get my feet on the ground. His mom is wonderful."

"I am so glad to hear it." Paige paused. "Sam, I am calling on a legal matter and was wondering if you or Michael can help me out?"

"What can we do?"

"Well I have been fostering a young girl for the last four months. Your dad is letting her ride Piper out at my parents' place."

"Yeah, it sounds like she is doing wonderfully with him. I am so happy he has someone to play with," Sam said.

"Well…" Paige relayed the story all the way to the phone call this morning.

Sam was quiet for a moment, thinking. "Let me check with Michael and see what he has to say, alright?" The baby started crying in the background.

"I would sure appreciate it," Paige said. "They want me to pack her things and take her down to the DHS office on Tuesday."

"Are you sure this is what you want, Paige?"

"I haven't talked to Abby, but if she is willing and thinks it would be good, I think we could make it work."

"I will call you a little later today. Let's see if we can do something."

"Talk to you later, Sam. I sure appreciate it." Paige hung up the phone and sighed.

She walked to the bathroom and started the shower. As she undressed, she noticed evidence from the night before. Her body tingled. *One thing at a time*, she thought. She caught her breath. She could feel him. She put her hand on her necklace to take it off, and she felt for the clasp. She closed her eyes. She could hear his voice, '*Make a wish.*' She gently rubbed the crucifix in her hand, and a feeling of completeness filled her.

His words echoed in her mind. *"I can't imagine any other place I want to be, or anyone else that I want to share it with."* She stepped into the shower.

20

Craig woke up in the aftermath of the previous night. It had only been four hours since he had dropped off Paige. He could feel her next to him for a moment in memory of the evening before. It felt like a dream, but the reality of it—what the heck? He felt like a teenager. He had really wanted to stay with her but thought better of it. His dad was going to gather cows by five thirty in the morning. He didn't want to have to answer a bunch of questions, so with a heavy heart, he had dropped Paige off at midnight. He walked her to the door with intense determination, gave her a kiss goodnight, got in his jeep, and drove away.

The air around the barnyard was invigorating. There was a sense of completeness that filled him as he walked out to the barn. The morning light was gathering strength on the East horizon while the early birds were practicing their morning choir in the trees around the house. Craig grabbed a halter off the wall and headed to the corral, where four horses were casually munching hay. They all raised their heads and watched him. Craig chose the big bay horse his dad called Booger who turned his butt toward Craig and walked away to the far end of the corral. Craig followed and waited for him to stop. Booger made it to the corner, decided there was no place else to go, and turned to face him. Craig walked up and laid the lead line over his neck, Booger dropped his nose down for the halter then followed Craig to the barn. The big horse ate grain while Craig got his brush and gave quick short strokes with the soft bristles, lifting dirt from where the saddle was to go.

Jim looked at his son as he passed. "Looks like you're a little late this morning," he chided, heading to the haystack. His horse, Mouse, was already saddled and had eaten his grain.

"Yeah, kind of a late night last night," Craig answered.

Jim had a pitchfork full of hay heading out to feed the few bummer calves in the off pasture. As he opened the gate, the calves gathered around him. He poured a little vitamin supplement on the hay and watched as they pushed and butted around until everyone had their place. "Better than grain," Jim said as he walked back into the barn.

Craig was wiping the dust off his double-rigged buckaroo saddle.

Jim looked at the big bay horse and grinned. "I haven't ridden him in a while, Craig. You might want to watch yourself today."

Craig grinned back. "I need a good challenge today, Dad." He checked his cinch and leathers to make sure if he did have a buck, it wouldn't be the saddle's fault if he landed on the ground.

"Just don't go daydreaming on him," his father warned.

"He will have my full attention." Craig grinned.

"Yeah, I bet," Jim said as he untied his grulla horse. "Just need you in the saddle, son."

Craig untied Booger and followed his dad to the trailer. He walked past a wall peg and grabbed Booger's cricket roller bit bridle. "That will give you something to think about." He stroked the horse's neck and pointed his nose into the trailer. Booger hopped in and Craig closed the tailgate.

He jogged back to the barn, grabbed his chinks, headed back to the rig, and slid into the passenger side of the pickup. He looked at his father and grinned.

His dad handed him a cup of coffee. "You're looking mighty chipper this morning. Did you have a good time last night?"

Craig took the large cup, "Thanks, I think I need this today." He took a sip, looked down at his jeans then back up at his dad. "I had a real good time, Dad."

"Good," Jim said as he put the Dodge in gear and pulled out of the driveway.

They rode in silence across town. The dawn was changing from passionate pink to gold and yellows as they started climbing up out of Baker Valley into the rolling sagebrush hills. They passed Ruckles Creek Road that could have taken them to Paige's old house then past the Keating turn off road.

Memories flooded Craig's mind of the day his mother had taken him out to the Cason place to give Paige her awards she had won at the horse show ten years ago. It seemed so long ago and yet just like yesterday. He remembered every detail, lying under the weeping willow, spending the afternoon looking at her artwork, watching Abe work a colt, and helping him put in a fence post. He remembered sitting at the dinner table and the family saying grace. But the one memory that was so vivid in his mind was, sitting on the porch telling Paige that he was moving to New York, then his first kiss. That was a long time ago, yet the thought took him back to last night—the swim, the dinner, lying under the stars, and never wanting the night to end.

Jim stopped the truck at a gate just off the main road. Craig was brought back to reality. "We are going to gather this bunch of pairs and put them on the old Whitman place. It shouldn't take us more than a couple hours," Jim said as he waited for Craig to get out of the truck.

Craig nodded as he opened the door, stepped out and silently opened the wire gate. Jim pulled through and parked away from the fence.

Craig grabbed his chinks and put the leather leggings on, buckling them behind his legs. He grabbed his leather gloves and slipped them in between the leather strap and his jeans' front pocket. Grabbing his bridle, he headed to the back of the trailer. As he unlatched the door, the big ole horse hopped out for him. Craig knew he was home. This is what he wanted to do. He subconsciously checked Booger's cinch and pulled it up a little tighter.

"Alright, big boy, let's go for a ride," he said as he slipped the bridle and his rawhide braided bozal over his nose, and tucked his 'get down rope' in his belt. Booger dropped his head and took the cricket bit easily. He played with the copper roller with his tongue to moisten his mouth. Craig turned him in a couple of circles to loosen him up a little, like he would a colt, before he got on. Then with his left rein hand placed securely on Booger's withers, he put his foot in the stirrup. He grabbed the saddle horn with his right hand as he swung easily into the saddle and had his right foot in the off stirrup before the horse could think about it. Booger waited patiently for Craig to get seated with no worry or tension.

Jim turned his mouse-colored horse around a couple of times and dipped his left elbow inside the rein by the neck. With his hand on the withers, he tipped Mouse's head around, put his other hand on the saddle horn, then stepped aboard the same way. The colt's head was high, his back was tight, and he was looking for a reason to move forward. Jim didn't wait around and let the young horse move forward with no tension or restrictions from the rider. Jim had been on enough horses to know this youngster was not looking for trouble. He was just uncertain of what Jim wanted him to do. Forward motion was far better in Jim's mind than the up and down motion of bucking. Let the little guy figure it out one step at a time. He would be tired by the time they got back to the truck and would find his pace.

"Let's air these guys out," Jim said as he rode Mouse past Craig. Mouse was moving out quickly and steadily.

Craig felt Booger's back tighten into a hump under the saddle. He fixed his hat down tight on his head and rearranged his lariat tethered securely to the pommel next to the saddle horn. He turned the horse into a circle to loosen him up a little then followed his dad. He was hoping for a smooth ride, but Booger took about twenty strides, slammed on his breaks, dropped his head between his front legs, and went to bucking. He took a gulp of air and let it out in a bellow. Craig grabbed for his lariat and held on.

Jim heard the commotion and stopped Mouse. He turned to watch his son ride. Booger got about ten good jumps in, at one point kicking his heels over Craig's head, but Craig held fast. He moved his legs like riding a bronc to help keep his balance. Booger squalled again, made a couple more jumps, then lined out and headed in the direction of the rising sun, as if nothing happened. His long legs were reaching well under himself to cover the ground. Craig kept a hold of the lariat for a little while in case Booger decided to give it another go.

Mouse hopped around with the excitement but Jim held his nose with one rein. When Craig got lined out, Jim let Mouse have his head as they set out. He asked as they rode past, "Got the kinks out?"

"Thinking so," Craig replied. They had four hundred acres of open land to ride to find eighty cow-calf pairs. "If not, should have them out by the time we get back to the truck."

Jim grinned at his son. It was good to have Craig home.

The cows gathered easily. As soon as they saw a horse, they started calling for their calves and moving together. The cowboys took their time to give them plenty of time to find their calves and head out.

Jim hollered, "Yip, yip, yip. Take your babies and go, mamas. Take your babies and go."

Craig started for the other side of the large meadow, nudging Booger into a long jog. "Yip, yip," he hollered as he went. Booger had lined out pretty fast, happy to do something besides stand in the pasture. He seemed to like Craig, who was an honest easy ride on his back.

The cows seemed happy to be moving as they gathered and moved forward with ease. Jim rode past Craig. "Take them easy as we go down. There is a narrow trail we will let them pick their way down."

"Alright, they look like they know where they are going."

"They do," Jim said as he jogged on ahead to turn a couple of replacement heifers.

The cows slowed down as one by one they gathered at the head of the drop off with their babies at their sides. There on the edge of the meadow, a singlewide trail headed down over the sheer rock bluff. Jim knew to keep everyone mothered up they needed to take their time and not push them too hard as they casually walked down the narrow trail. Jim took advantage of the waiting and headed over a little knoll to see if any were hiding in the dips of the pasture. He had ridden this place so many times he knew where the mamas would hide their babies and wanted to make sure none would be left behind. He found an aged cow that had hidden her baby under a clump of brush.

Mouse shied away from her as he rounded the bunch of brush thinking the cow looked like a black bear. He jumped to the side as the mama turned and jumped at him, protecting her baby.

"Hey, mama! Here, here!" Jim called to her, trying to steady his mount as the young horse jumped again. Jim let the unsure colt move around as he guided him around the buck brush again. The mama ragged her head and bellowed at the intruder of horse and rider. He circled again and slapped his chink leggings with the end of his rawhide rein. The calf jumped up out of the brush and ran to his mama. Mouse's head was high and nervous, and his ears were twitching back and forth. He felt his rider's confidence but anticipated an attack from a mooing bear-looking cow.

Jim worked his way around the brush for the third time and the old cow gave a soft call to her calf. She released her anchor of protection and with calf tucked tightly at her side, she headed in the direction of the herd.

"Take your baby and go, mama. Take your baby and go," Jim said quietly as he pulled Mouse to a stop and watched her walk away. He knew if he followed too closely, it would cause the cow to want to fight instead of travel. All he had to do was keep an eye on her so she wouldn't turn and try to hide again or make an escape in the opposite direction.

As the last of the cows made their way to the bottom of the bluff, Craig headed Booger to the edge of the cliff and looked down, seeing the moving cows about sixty yards below. "Oh boy! " He sighed as he felt dizziness overtake him. He took a breath. "Well, mister, this is where I have to trust you, my friend." He stroked Booger's neck.

Craig looked below at the cows continuing their journey through the rocky washout. "Well if they can do it, we can do it," he said as he gave Booger his head. The horse moved out easily like he had done this before, not even hesitating at the rugged edge and height. After he got started down about a quarter of the way, Craig pulled Booger to a stop. Just before him, was a hairpin corner with a bulging rock that stuck out to just over Craig's head. It rounded out and rolled back into the cliff just about knee high. The cows walked just under that bulging rock, but with Booger's size and Craig up on his back, he was trapped on the narrow path with nowhere to turn back. And no way for him to get past that rock without leaning his body out over the sheer edge and lifting his leg out of the stirrup and over Booger's shoulder. Booger stepped forward with confidence, and Craig held him up trying to contemplate the predicament he was in. Booger bobbed his head asking for forward motion. Craig took a breath and respected the horse's wishes. Booger moved forward freely, and Craig pulled his leg in front of the groove of the horse's shoulder. In a subtle motion Booger swayed his back as Craig leaned his body completely over the saddle lying flat as he could on the horse's neck. With a soft brush of pant leg to rock, Booger never missed a step as he carried Craig the rest of the way down the narrow path following quietly behind the cows.

Craig had to grin as he stroked Booger's neck in appreciation of a good horse. Booger cocked back an ear at his rider.

Jim continued following the old cow as she took her calf where Booger had just been. Craig waited at the bottom as the cow caught up with the rest. What he would do for a coffee right now. He watched his dad take the young horse down the narrow trail. He watched as his dad lifted his leg the same as he had and leaned forward on the saddle. The young horse followed the feeling with confidence and trust as he continued around the hairpin and walked up next to Craig. Jim stepped off Mouse and loosened the cinch for a few moments. He resituated the blanket and let the colt's back air out a little before cinching him back up.

"Guess I will ride point and let you follow them on out, Craig. I want to make sure they get turned into the fence line and get down to the corner gate."

Craig nodded. They would shift from side to side once in a while letting the tail end come along slowly and easily. As long as the cows were in motion, they didn't need to be pushed.

The cows were put into the old Whitman place by ten thirty. There was plenty of grass and water to get them through the summer and an easy gather in the fall down at the lower corrals.

Craig had to smile at his dad as he sidestepped Booger up to the wire-fenced gate and grabbed the gate pole. Booger stepped through the opened gate and waited as Craig fumbled a little to latch it shut. They had mothered the cows, just to make sure no calves were left behind. All the mamas were quiet, but the two men sat at the fence and watched as the cows lined out and fed on new grass with calves close at their sides. Other babies lay down to take a rest.

Craig and Jim both turned their horses and headed back to the trailer. The horses' heads were swinging in rhythm of their feet. Jim's jingle bobs on his spurs made music to Mouse's walking rhythm. It seemed to calm the nervousness in the young horse to have something to listen to. Mouse didn't like the quiet so much. A doe and her fawn stood on the skyline watching the two men with cautious alertness. Frozen in their tracks, they waited for the men to pass over fifty yards away. Mouse kept his eye on the two aliens, but sensing no tension from his rider, kept moving forward. An hour later they rode up to the truck and trailer. Jim and Craig both stepped off their sweat-dried horses and loosened their cinches. They took off their bridles and slipped the halters on before they loaded them in the trailer, then got into the cab of the truck.

Craig reached in the back of the truck and pulled out a jug of water. "I forgot how dry a feller can get riding for cows," he said as he handed the jug to his dad.

"You get to where you don't notice it," his dad replied as he took a swig and handed it back to Craig. "Sure appreciate you helping me today, son. Why don't we stop by the Truck Stop and get us some lunch before we head home."

"Glad I am here, Dad. I wouldn't miss it for the world. Sounds great, I'm starved."

There was silence as they pulled out onto the road and headed back toward town then Jim spoke up, "So when is your flight leaving?"

"I have got to be in Boise around eight o'clock on Wednesday," he said halfheartedly. "I don't really want to go. I am thinking I could move back here and help out around the ranch and do a little contracting."

Jim looked at him. "All I can say, son, is do what your heart tells you. Life is too short to waste it on things you are not passionate about." He paused for a moment then said, "But I don't think I need to tell you that. I think you might even know that a little more than me."

Craig nodded in agreement, yet he knew his dad had seen so many things in his lifetime that he never talked about, from the death of animals to divorce. He would take his advice out of respect.

21

Paige drove out to her parents' house. She grabbed a cup of coffee and sat at the table as her mother and Abby worked at getting green beans in the jars.

Abby was beaming. "When we get done with all of the canning, we are going to take the rest down to the farmer's market and sell it. I can't wait."

Patricia smiled.

Paige remembered snapping beans and canning just like they were doing now. She smiled at the memory. Noticing a full bowl of green beans sitting in front of her, she grabbed one and started breaking them in three pieces. She grabbed another and subconsciously began snapping beans and drinking coffee. How could she take this away from Abby?

Patricia looked at her, "Rough night?"

"No, but this morning is pretty tough." Paige sighed. "Abby, can you go outside for a few moments and let me talk to Mom for a second?"

"Sure, Paige. Are you ok?"

"Yeah, I am fine. Just need to talk to my mom."

"Come on, Blue," Abby said as she dropped the last beans in the jar and tapped it down. They walked out the door together, Blue's red scarf still tied around her neck like a collar.

Patricia came and sat down across from her daughter. "What's going on, Paige?"

"I got a phone call this morning." Paige paused. "Department of Human Services wants to place Abby in a troubled girls' school."

"What? They can't do that. Not now. Not when she has come so far," Patricia said.

"Mom, a few weeks ago, I went to them and told them that my position with Abby was as a temporary foster care. After four months of her living here, she was being completely withdrawn from life and all things around her. Something needed to be done." Paige paused. "They told me at that time that they had six more weeks of scheduled therapy and a change of medication they wanted to try on her."

Patricia listened intently. "Yes."

"Well, I told them she didn't need medication. She needed a reason to live, and at that time I didn't think I could give it to her." Paige stopped again. "I requested that they take her back." Paige paused. "I never took her to the therapist to get evaluated." Tears started forming in Paige's eyes. She blinked them back. "They want me to bring her in with all her belongings day after tomorrow."

Paige looked out the window at Abby throwing a stick for Blue. Patricia followed her gaze and watched as Blue ran after the stick in flight.

"So what are you thinking, Paige?"

"I am thinking of adopting her," Paige answered. "I can't stand to think of Abby going into a school until she is eighteen where everything she does is evaluated and manipulated into what the system thinks is healthy or not. I want to know what you think."

Paige grabbed another bean, snapped it and put it with the others.

"I think you would be a good mother to her, or mentor, and she seems so happy to be a part of what we do."

Abe walked through the door.

"Babe," Patricia said, "come and sit down and listen to what Paige has to say."

Paige looked at her father, took a breath and one more time relayed the conversation that she had with Ben on the phone. When she had finished that story, she continued that she had called Samantha that morning and was thinking about adopting Abby.

"She deserves better than a school, doesn't she? I know that there is only ten years' difference in our age," Paige argued trying to make a case for her. "But I have to at least try. I know it will be tough to pull things together, but you guys did it. I can do it too, can't I?" Paige questioned, then went silent so her parents could think.

Abe looked over at Patricia, then back at Paige. "My girls," he said. He paused and looked back at Patricia.

"You know, Paige," he said, "life is a funny thing. Things just seem to line up before you. Even through the darkest hours, somehow things work out." He paused for a second. "I know how much this girl means to you. Your mom and I are pretty smitten too. If you want to try to adopt her, we surely wouldn't stand in your way. But if you choose not to, your mother and I were talking about maybe adding her to our family."

Paige was silent as she put the pieces together. "You want to adopt Abby?"

"Well, we have talked about it for the last couple of days. We didn't know what you would think about it, but while you were in the hospital and she stayed out here with us, we realized that she needs a place to call home. If you want to put in the papers, Patricia and I will back you all the way. If not, we would like to get the paperwork started. We didn't realize how much we missed having a kid running around."

A tear ran down Paige's cheek, "That means I would have a little sister."

"And we would have another child." Patricia beamed. "Abe and I are ready to check with Abby and see if that is what she wants too. If you are ok with it, Paige."

"I am so ok with it." She looked back out the window at a young girl who had been through so much, now hopefully coming home. Piper had walked up, putting his head over the fence to watch the girl throwing the stick for Blue. Abby saw him and walked over to stroke his nose.

Patricia called Abby in. She was only using one crutch now and seemed to cover the ground by leaps and bounds. Blue bounded after her, bouncing up and down for the stick she held over her head as she walked.

Abby sat down at the table and looked at the three people in her life. Blue went to Paige and put her head on her lap, looking at her with her piercing blue eyes.

"Abby," Patricia started, then paused. "We are wondering…" She stopped again. "Abby, Abe and I want to know if you would want to join our family and let us adopt you?"

Abby looked at Paige then back at Patricia and Abe.

Patricia continued, "Now it is not a for sure thing, Abby, but we want you to think about it. That would mean you would no longer be Abigail Marie Sorenson. You would be Abigail Marie Cason. It would put your old life to rest and start a new life with us. All this does is change your name but not who you are, Abby. Does this make sense?"

Abby looked over the table at Paige, then said, "That would make you my sister."

"Your big sister," Paige said with tears in her eyes.

"Abigail Cason," Abby thought for a moment. "I don't like it," she said defiantly.

Patricia glanced at Abe, but they said nothing.

"Abby Cason. I like it. I really like it." She repeated it again, "Abby Cason."

Then reality hit her and tears started to form in her eyes. "Does this mean I have to forget my real parents?"

Abe spoke up, "No, you will never forget them. They are the ones who brought you to us." He looked at her then got up and gave her a hug.

Her frame fell into his fatherly arms and she cried.

22

Charlie Thomas looked in the pickup mirror. He had shaved earlier that day just before daylight and wanted to make sure he hadn't missed any spots. His worn out cowboy hat covered his lengthening hair and he had put on one of his t-shirts he had washed in the Snake River just before he crossed over into Oregon. It was going to be a long day, and he didn't have time to be messing around.

He looked over at the door of the Truck Corral Restaurant. He had eighty-two dollars and seventy-nine cents in his pocket. His stomach growled with anticipation as his mind contemplated splurging for some real food. He had been living off peanut butter and jelly sandwiches and chili for the last five days. The smell of freshly made coffee was making him feel weak. If he got an omelet and hash browns he could make it last three days, he calculated in his head. He reached in his pocket and fumbled with the small roll of bills. The gas pump was still running. He walked around his single axle horse trailer and checked the bald tires. His pickup truck with his bedroll and a mare heavy with foal was all he had left of his old life. He lost the rest in foreclosure after losing his wife to cancer. They took everything including the kitchen sink.

Sleeping out next to the freeway for the last couple of nights didn't seem to bother him or his dog Flick. He would unload the old mare to give her some time to rest on solid ground, tether her at night, pitch his little camp, and listen to semi-trucks and fast-paced cars traveling to busy places.

He really didn't have anywhere to go. He was heading for Washington, up in the Tri-City area, where his wife's brother lived, hoping for a little company and a place to stay until he got back on his feet. That wasn't really very promising because the two never really did see eye to eye on things. But it was at least some place to go. He was tired of feeling like everyone judged him or took pity on him. *Nobody understood*, he thought as he had left his hometown. But as he put distance to old memories and friends, he was beginning to think maybe they understood a little more than what he gave them credit for.

The old Plaudit mare shifted uncomfortably in the trailer. It was pretty tight quarters for a mare to be traveling, but he couldn't bear to sell her. She was the first and the last of his little band of broodmares. She was packing a colt out of a son of King's Pistol. The last of Charlie's dreams of his old life with old bloodlines. He reached in the trailer and soothed her for a moment. "Easy, girl, I will get you out in a few minutes." She needed a place to stay for a while. She was not going to take too many more days of traveling.

The gas pump shut off, and he looked at the price. He would wait on the coffee and omelet.

He pulled out his small wad of bills, paid the attendant, and counted what he had left. He carefully folded them and put them back in his pocket. He slid in the driver's seat and started the engine. As he'd promised, he pulled around the parking lot where the semi-trucks parked. There was a stock trailer with two horses in it, so he parked next to it and let down the tail ramp for the mare to step out. Milk was running down her legs and Charlie was almost sick.

"Not now, mama, please not now," he begged as he wondered where to go from there.

Charlie heard two men talking.

"If we leave by four that will get us there by seven at the latest, that would be eight their time," Craig said as he calculated an hour for the time change. They came around the back end of the stock trailer.

Jim noticed a middle-aged man leading a nice buckskin horse around the trailer. "Mornin," he said toward the stranger.

"Morning," Charlie replied.

"Everything alright?" Jim asked looking at the heavy mare.

Charlie looked over at them then looked at his horse. He was at the end of the line. "No, don't think so."

"Where you headed?"

"Was headed to Washington but I don't think I am going to get there." Without thinking Charlie asked, "Do you know anyplace that a man can house a horse around here? I don't have any money and this mare isn't going to make it."

Jim saw the strained look on the stranger's face. He looked at the buckskin again. Milk had dripped down both hind legs.

"Do you want to take her to a vet?" Craig asked a little concerned for the situation that the man was in.

"If I did, I wouldn't be able to pay them," the stranger said. "She is the last thing I have and I think I am going to lose her if I don't do something quick. I will work it out in trade if someone has a place to hold her for a while."

"Well, mister, I have a place just outside of town here if you want to bring her out to our place or," Jim thought for a moment, " there is a friend of mine who boards horses and might be better suited for her about twelve miles from here. Let me give them a call and see if they have some room."

Jim walked up to the pay phone and called the Casons.

Patricia answered the phone.

"Hey, Patricia, this is Jim. Say I have a feller here who has a mare about ready to foal and he needs a place for her. He said he would work to pay for her board. Patricia," Jim paused, "he is needing a place now."

She took the hint and knew that if Jim was calling it was a pretty serious situation.

"Jim, have him bring her out. I will get a place set up for her. I will let Abe know."

"We will be right over." He hung up the phone.

He looked over at the stranger. "My name is Jim Curry, and we have a place we can put your mare for a while. Can you load her up?"

"Charlie Thomas." He held out his hand to Jim, giving a firm handshake to the big man. "I will see if I can get her back in the trailer." He led her to the back of the old trailer ramp. She looked at the ramp and hesitated.

Jim couldn't watch it. The mare's sides were heavy with a colt that had already dropped. She looked like she would foal within the next twenty-four hours. "Say, Charlie, why don't you load her in the stock trailer and I will take you out to the Cason place."

Craig opened up the back of the stock trailer, pushed Mouse and Booger up to the front and shut the center divider. Jim held the door open and Charlie looked at him for a moment. He knew he could do no more for this mare and had to trust that things would be alright. He led her to the back of the stock trailer, and without hesitation, she stepped in. Charlie tied her to the side panel and stepped out as Jim shut the door.

"Just follow us out toward Haines. I think it will be a good place for her to be."

Charlie went and raised the tail ramp to his old trailer and latched it into place. He felt alone without the old mare in there.

His border collie dog, Flick, wagged his tail as he approached the front of the truck and got in. "Well,

Flick, looks like we are on another adventure," he said as he started his truck and followed the stock trailer down Campbell Street through Baker City and out toward the little town of Haines.

As he followed them, Charlie thought it was odd how not more than three years ago he was riding cutting horses and starting to make a name for himself. Had a wife, he started making a little money, bought his own little ranch and a new truck and trailer. Now here he was, relying on total strangers to help him out.

Twenty minutes later they pulled up at the Cason place and Patricia met them in the driveway. Jim pulled up next to the barn and stopped the truck. Craig jumped out and headed for the trailer. They were unloading the mare as Charlie pulled in.

"Hey, Jim," Patricia said as she walked down to the barn, "let's put her in here for now."

"Hi, Patricia, this is Charlie Thomas. He owns this mare," Jim said as Charlie got out of his truck and walked down to where they were leading the mare. Flick stuck his head out the driver's side window, his tongue lolling out to the side.

Charlie looked at a blonde woman walking toward him. She walked with a sense of purpose and confidence.

He took Patricia's small, callused hand and shook it. "Nice to meet you. I sure appreciate you taking us in like this. I was hoping to make it up to Washington before she decided to have this guy, but you know Mother Nature, she has a mind of her own."

"Nice to meet you, Charlie. Let's put her in Shorty's corner stall with the paddock so she can move around a little bit. Craig, I just put fresh sawdust in there."

"Alright, Mrs. Cason." His respect for her stronger than her want of calling her by her first name, Craig corrected himself. "Patricia," Craig said as he led the mare.

Jim walked over with Charlie and Patricia asked, "So Charlie, what is in Washington?"

"Well I have a brother-in-law there that I was going to stay with until I got back on my feet, but things are not looking too good for me right now. Been camped out on the freeway for the last couple of days and was hoping to make a last push to Washington today to get her some relief from traveling before she foaled."

"When she due?"

"In a week."

"You're cutting it pretty close."

"Well sometimes you can't choose your circumstances.

You just have to go with what you got." He wasn't wanting to get into his story.

"Boy I understand that," Jim said as they stopped at the stall and watched Craig turn the mare loose.

Charlie looked over at Patricia. "Mrs. Cason, I don't know what I can do to pay you. I am a pretty good hand and will do you right if given the opportunity. I was wondering if I could stay here with my mare for a few days. I got my bedroll out in the truck and I promise not to be a bother."

Jim hadn't heard anyone talk like that in a long time and was wondering what the story was on Charlie. Jim looked again and realized Charlie was a lot younger than what he'd originally thought.

Patricia saw the hollow look in his eyes, the bony cheeks, and leather-like face. "Charlie, I will talk to my husband and see if we can work something out. But for right now as this mare settles in, why don't we get you something to eat."

"That is alright, Mrs. Cason, but could I ask for some water for my dog? I have my own food in the truck."

"Well, let me see. I have water for your dog and I have roast beef sandwiches, potato salad, and canned peaches if you would like."

Charlie was quiet too long to decline.

"There is a spigot for water to the left of the barn door there." Patricia pointed toward the swinging door. "I will go and get you some food. Jim, did you and Craig already eat?" Patricia asked as she walked toward the house.

"We did, Patricia. I am sorry to say, we did."

"Do you drink coffee, Charlie?"

"Yes ma'am." Charlie watched her walk away. She had a purpose about her that made him feel like he could not decline.

"Be back in a minute," Patricia called over her shoulder.

"She doesn't need to do that," Charlie said to Jim watching her walk away.

"You don't say no to Patricia's cooking. Actually, you don't say no to Patricia," Jim said with a grin.

Craig tossed some grass hay in the stall for the mare and leaned on the top rail looking at her. "She is a pretty nice mare," he said as he watched her.

Charlie looked over at his buckskin, who had walked across the corral and was getting a drink. "Yeah, she has been a good mare. I sure like her." The mare kicked at her belly with her hind foot.

He looked at Jim then back a Craig. "You guys sure didn't have to do this, but I sure appreciate it." Charlie felt his throat tighten up as if he would cry.

"Abe and Patricia are good people. So what do you do Charlie?" Jim asked as he leaned on the rail with Craig.

"I ranched most all of my life. Lost my wife to cancer and lost everything I had. This ole mare was my wife's favorite, and I kind of wanted to keep her. But I am thinking maybe it ain't in the cards."

"Sure sorry to hear about your wife," Jim said a little concerned of the topic.

Charlie looked over at him. "She has got to be in a better place than where she was. She put up a hell of a fight." He paused. "Sometimes you just have to let go."

Craig looked at him for the first time with a deep understanding. Charlie looked older than his years.

"Say you don't know of anyone who needs a hired hand for a while, do you? I could sure use a job."

Jim looked at him for a minute, "Can you build fence?"

"I can build fence, weld, mechanic, and swath hay. I can ride and rope. I guess you would call me a jack of all trades." He grinned. "How does it go? Master of none."

Patricia came out with a platter full of sandwiches, potato salad, plates, forks, peaches, and a thermos of coffee, all in a basket. She put it down on the table next to the barn entrance. "You boys should probably eat something," she said as she started laying it out. "Abe will be here in a few minutes."

Patricia took two half sandwiches, a spoon of potato salad, and two peach halves and handed the plate to Charlie. He set it down in front of him and she poured a cup of coffee for him.

Charlie looked at the food and once more said almost embarrassed, "I can't pay you."

They looked at each other for a moment. "Eat," Patricia said as she walked away.

He sat down at the table trying to remember his table manners and took a bite of the roast beef sandwich. It felt like it melted in his mouth. He closed his eyes and savored the moment. It seemed that in less than three bites the half of sandwich was gone. The smell of the coffee wafted his direction, and he took the cup in his hand. The warmth seemed to soothe him. Charlie hesitated then took a sip. It felt like he had died and gone to heaven.

Jim took a half of sandwich and so did Craig. They sat next to Charlie. "There is nothing like Patricia's cooking,"

Craig said as he bit into his half of sandwich.

Abe came around the barn on his bay horse, Cricket. "Hey, Jim, Craig, how are you doing?"

Charlie got up from the table and looked at Abe while trying to swallow the rest of his sandwich. Abe stepped off his horse and loosened his cinch.

Jim introduced them. "Abe Cason, this is Charlie Thomas. He has run into a little trouble and needed a place to keep his mare until she foals."

Abe saw the weathered look of Charlie and looked into his eyes as they shook hands. There was an honesty there that Abe seemed to notice. "Good to meet you, Charlie."

"Thank you, sir. Good to meet you too. Mr. Cason, I have already told your wife and I will tell you. I have no way to pay you right now but I will do what I can to make it right with you." There was a grounded quality in his words—total honesty and trust.

Abe noticed these were not easy words to say to a total stranger. Charlie looked him straight in the eyes and said what needed to be said. "Where you staying?" Abe asked, as he saw the half-eaten sandwich on the table.

"Well I would like to stay with my mare if I could. I have a bedroll and food in the truck. I promise not to be any trouble."

Abe looked over at Patricia as she returned with more coffee, then Jim. There was a look about Charlie that gave Abe that feeling of a man at the end of his rope. It was all too familiar. Abe had been there with Patricia and Paige. "Tell you what, Charlie. If you stay, I will have you help out around here."

"I will do what I can."

Charlie looked over at the sandwich sitting on the table, wanting to finish it but not wanting to be rude.

Abe took the gesture in kind and reached over to grab a sandwich and a plate. "Go ahead and finish your lunch. We will talk in a few minutes."

They all sat around the picnic table and talked quietly of introductions. As Jim finished his sandwich, he stood up. "Patricia, I can never turn down your food. Thank you for the sandwich and coffee, it beats the heck out of truck stop food."

Patricia grinned at him. "Jim you know you are welcome any time."

Patricia had made it back to the house with her basket of lunch leftovers. She left two half sandwiches wrapped in plastic wrap next to Charlie's belongings. There was a lot of planning to do. And she was pretty excited to have a mare about ready to foal too. She anticipated Abby being thrilled to see a newborn colt. She put the dishes in the sink and ran some dishwater.

With the help of Samantha and Michael, she prayed that the adoption of Abby would go smoothly. The thought of having Abby as a part of the family was fresh and invigorating. What a change in life it would be.

"Well, Charlie," Jim said, "if you can build fence, I could sure use some help tomorrow if Abe doesn't have anything for you to do."

Abe thought for a moment and said, "I don't see any reason why he couldn't, Jim. We can watch the mare and see what happens tonight."

"Yes sir, I would sure appreciate the work," Charlie said excitedly.

"I will pick you up at seven then," Jim said as he looked over at Craig then Abe.

"I will be ready."

"Well, we had better be heading home. If you need anything, Abe, give us a call."

"You bet, Jim, I will give you a holler," Abe said as he sat next to Patricia and put a little potato salad on his plate.

Charlie felt a little uncomfortable for a moment.

"So tell me about your mare," Abe said as he poured a cup of coffee and settled into eating his lunch.

Charlie looked at him for a moment and began. "Well she is a granddaughter out of Plaudit. I had her bred to a son of King's Pistol stud. I can't find any better breeding, and she has thrown me some really nice colts."

Abe was interested. "So what brings you into this country?"

Charlie took a breath then started to tell a little about his story and how he had been working cutting horses and started his own little herd. How he sold them off one by one when his wife got sick and lost the rest to foreclosure right after she passed.

"Not a lot a feller can do when he loses everything except keep putting one foot in front of the other," Charlie said quietly.

"Been there about fifteen, sixteen years ago," Abe said as he listened to the story. He got up to change the mood, walked over to Cricket and began to unsaddle him. Charlie got up and followed, interested in the young bay horse standing quietly.

His experienced eye told him he was a well-bred horse and he wanted to know more. But he waited for Abe to offer the information. Abe didn't.

"You have many horses like this one?" Charlie asked.

"I have two geldings, out of my stud, the rest are horses that I ride for other people," Abe answered as he grabbed a brush from the tack room. He looked at Charlie and could see that he knew his horses.

Abe usually worked alone, but since Charlie was looking to work off the boarding, he offered him the brush. Abe would just as well see how he could handle a horse. Charlie hesitated a second, accepted the brush, then approached the young horse.

Charlie untied him and led him away from the hitching post. Abe was surprised. He knew that if the colt was unfamiliar with Charlie, the horse might jump back away from him and start pulling on the rope.

Untying the young horse and leading him around a moment gave them a chance to read each other before Charlie started brushing.

Abe liked him. He was quiet, kind, and knowledgeable.

"He is out of my stud, Shorty," Abe said.

"He is a nice guy," Charlie replied as he stroked down his back with the soft bristled brush.

"I have a cutting this next weekend and want to keep him fresh."

Charlie beamed at the thought.

They talked like old friends. Abe found they had a lot in common as they chatted through the afternoon. Finally Abe said, "You know, Charlie, I will let you get settled in. Are you sure you don't want to stay in the house? We have an extra bed."

"No thanks I will just throw my bedroll out here in the barn and keep an eye on my mare. Sure appreciate your hospitality though."

They got up and walked back into the barn to look at the mare. She was resting easily in the middle of the stall, her eyes half closed.

"Dinner is at six," Abe said as he headed for the house.

23

Craig was anxious to call Paige when he got home at two thirty, but no one answered. He didn't leave a message. He jumped in the shower to soak his sore tired body, and then turned on the cold water to bring himself back to life.

He threw on a clean pair of jeans and a white t-shirt, jumped in his jeep, and headed to Paige's. No one was home. He left a note on the door.

Dropped by to see you, thinking of you.

Craig

He thought about wadding it up, but then thought better of it and found some old tape in the jockey box of the jeep to tape it to the door. Afterward, he headed for town. He had some friends he wanted to see while still here. He made a few phone calls and got a hold of an old friend from high school, Toby, who he agreed to meet at a bar. Toby had already had a couple of straight shots and a beer. Craig sat next to him and ordered a beer too. They started going over old times.

They talked about rodeo and bronc riding and drinking too much, then the topic turned to girls. Craig asked about some of the local girls and what they were doing. He talked about his wife Lisa.

Toby listened to Craig's story about his wife, "Yeah, I felt that way about a girl once."

"Really?" Craig asked. "And who was that?"

"Paige Cason," Toby said with a drawl of too much to drink. "Yep, I fell head over heels in love with her and she wouldn't have anything to do with me." He closed his eyes slowly, then opened them. "You know, I thought we hit it off pretty good when we were at John Greenly's place. We talked and laughed and had a good time. I asked her out a couple years ago," he thought for a moment, "and she agreed. I thought I had it in the bag." He stopped and winked at Craig. "If you know what I mean." He winked again. "We went out and had a couple of beers. I made a move on her," his words slurred, "and she was like a wild cat." He took another swallow of beer. "I thought she wanted it rough, and boy I was going to give it to her good." He grinned. "But, I ended up with a black eye and a bruised jaw for about two weeks." He finished his beer in one more gulp. "Yep, a wild cat, I tell you." He paused. "Hey," Toby hollered down the bar, "give us another round."

The barkeep looked down at Toby. "Nope, Tobe, you had your quota for the night."

"Oh bullshit, get us another round," he insisted.

"Hey," Craig said looking at Toby. "Why don't we call it a night? It has been a long day."

"You kidding me? The night is still young. If these assholes don't serve me another round I will go down the block." He kind of winked at Craig, like that was the trick to get another beer.

Craig noticed the difference in Toby and didn't want to be a part of it. He had seen it too many times.

"Well, bud, I am gonna have to go. I had a pretty long day." He had his second beer sitting on the counter. Craig pulled a ten out of his pocket and laid it on the bar to pay for his own beer and leave a tip.

Toby looked at Craig. "You gonna finish that?" He looked at the almost full beer.

"Nope, think I have had enough tonight," Craig replied.

Without even asking, he grabbed the beer and took

a gulp. "Haha, you bastards, see, told you I could get another one." He slurred as he leaned on the bar.

"Take care of yourself," Craig said as he patted Toby on the shoulder in a friendly gesture. He casually took the ten bucks off the bar and walked down to the bartender. "This is yours," he said, as he tapped the bar with his open hand. "Have a good evening."

Craig had seen too many guys like Toby, who at a certain point of drinking couldn't make a good choice if they wanted to. Talking about Paige like that was a shock. He was glad that she could handle herself. He really wanted to see her again. He thought about going back out to her house and seeing if she was home but thought better of it. With the smell of the bar and beer on his breath, that would be a conversation he wouldn't want to have with her. He drove out to the truck stop and ordered a Denver omelet for dinner.

Craig ate it in silence as he let his mind wander to all the day's excitement. Booger had him going there for a minute. A couple more jumps and he might have got him off. *Can't believe Dad still has some of those types of horses*, he thought. Meeting Charlie and hearing about the loss of his wife. His mind shifted back to his wife and a life he didn't belong to anymore. *Life is like a river forever flowing and always in motion*. Then he thought of Paige

Cason, and a smile found his lips. What was it about her that just lit him up every time he saw her or even thought of her? He thought of the previous night, her laughter, her words. He could still feel her hand run through his hair and her lips on his neck. A warmth filled his body. He took a sip of coffee. His eyes were heavy and his coffee strong. He paid his bill and headed home.

24

Charlie gathered his bedroll and Flick's bed and walked into the barn. He couldn't believe he was actually under a roof tonight and going to work in the morning. He walked over to the mare's stall and watched her eat. It felt good to smell the clean hay and to have something as simple as a roast beef sandwich and potato salad. He also enjoyed the conversation with like-minded people. *That doesn't happen very often,* he thought as he reached down and stroked Flick's head. He listened to the silence, not having cars and semi-trucks roaring past every thirty seconds or the exhaust fumes. Things seemed to be looking up.

He thought of three weeks prior when he left his home, his history, his life. His heart ached for the life he once had. The comfort of his wife's arms, the familiarity of the barn. The smell of the house. The simplicity of silly habits, the rockwork of the hearth he put in. Gone, no longer his to claim. He had to leave it. All that he had worked for, gone, sold at auction for some stranger to come and bid on. To put a price on one's life to pay unpaid medical bills of another one's death. He thought of taking his life. He didn't care if he went to hell or not. It couldn't be worse than driving away from everything you thought was yours and owning nothing but the shirt on your back and a bedroll.

The only way he kept the mare was by selling her to a good friend of his for a dollar. After the court proceedings, he was able to buy her back for a dollar. He thought of the one moment when he was driving blindly down the interstate as fast as he could go, passing anyone in his path hoping something would happen to make the pain and aloneness stop the only way he knew how. End it all and join his wife, but just before he turned his truck into the rear wheels of a semi-truck, Flick lifted his paw, put it on Charlie's arm and whined.

Charlie had looked at his dog for an instant and slowed his truck. Tears streamed down his face. His heart ached with emptiness and loneliness. He wanted it all to end, but he couldn't kill his dog over his own pain and he couldn't leave him behind without the only family he knew. He pulled off to the side of the road, laid his head on the steering wheel and cried.

Charlie squatted down and stroked the dog's head. "You kind of saved my life, my friend. You knew things would get better, didn't you?"

Flick put his paw on Charlie's leg. Charlie grinned as a tear ran down his cheek. "What an adventure. Huh, buddy?" He laid out his bedroll, straightened his blankets, and put Flick's bed next to his. He got out a notebook, sat down, and wrote in his journal:

Drove to Baker City this morning and met Jim and Craig Curry at truck stop. Plaudit is dripping milk and is close to foaling. Had first real meal in two weeks. Abe and Patricia Cason are housing us until foal arrives. Have a job. Good People.

He got out a book by Will James. He looked at the worn out cover as he read the title, *Cowboys North and South.* It had been his dad's book given to him by his Uncle Leo. He thought of the author that had been gone almost a hundred years, yet his stories still were alive within the pages. The old book fell open at his bookmark, and he began to read.

Charlie was up most all night. Every time Plaudit stamped a foot or swished a tail, he was wide awake checking on her. She constantly shifted her weight from one foot to the other looking to relieve the pressure the colt was putting on her. But there was no way to make herself comfortable. At six in the morning, Abe walked out to the barn to start doing chores. Charlie had found a wheelbarrow and pitchfork and was already mucking out the mare's stall.

"Mornin'."

"Mornin'. How is she doing?" Abe asked as he walked in the barn. Flick trotted over to him wagging his tail. Abe casually dropped his hand and stroked the dog's head.

"She is pretty uncomfortable," Charlie said. "I don't think she is going to wait until next week but I guess time will tell."

"Has she had any trouble foaling before?"

"No, usually she is right on schedule. Coming into her milk like she did yesterday made me a little nervous. It just might be the stress of traveling. I probably could have done things differently, but I didn't. Now here I am."

"How old are you, Charlie? If you don't mind me asking."

"Just turned thirty-eight."

Abe had guessed him to be in his mid to late forties. "Well, life has a tendency to give us a tough time once in a while. It is up to us on how we handle it. If it is worth anything to you and for what it is worth, I think you are handling it alright."

Abe grabbed his hayfork, stabbed four flakes of hay, and headed out the back side of the barn.

Charlie grabbed his manure fork and wheelbarrow and headed to the other paddock to clean it out as well. He thought of Abe's words. Half the time Charlie didn't know for sure what he was doing, but he kept trying to put one foot in front of the other. It was nice to think that in the mess of everything, someone thought he was doing alright. Even though in his own perspective he was lost as to where he was in his own life, he smiled to himself as he began to scrape the stall. For the first time in a long time, he felt comfortable, almost home.

***

After chores Patricia came out with a ham and cheese omelet and a thermos of coffee. "We thought you might want something to eat before you go to work this morning. Abe and I are going to be around all day today so we will keep an eye on your mare for you."

"I can't tell you how much this means to me," Charlie said. "You guys have been too kind, and I sure appreciate it."

"No worries," Abe said. "We have been in a similar situation and needed a little help too. Do what you need to."

Charlie looked at his plate. "I will bring the plate up to the house when I am done."

"Sounds good," Abe said as he turned to leave.

Charlie sat on a bale of hay, rested his plate on his legs, opened up the thermos, poured a cup of steaming hot coffee, and cut into an omelet he had so long been anticipating.

At seven o'clock, Jim pulled up with a stock trailer and two horses. "You have a saddle Charlie?"

"Yep." He answered without a second thought. He headed toward his pickup and grabbed his old Hamley's saddle out of the back with his two blankets and pad, then he headed toward Jim's truck. Charlie had a peanut butter sandwich and his thermos of coffee. He was ready for the day. Flick followed him to the truck, and Charlie looked at Jim with a question in his eyes.

"Does he chase cows?" Jim inquired, leery of having a strange stock dog around his cows.

"Only when I ask him to."

"As long as he doesn't bother them while we are working, you can bring him along."

Charlie motioned for Flick to get in on the floorboard. He lay down instantly and didn't move, just happy to be going with them. Charlie slipped in onto the passenger seat and closed the door.

"You ridden in this country before, Charlie?" Jim asked as he pulled out, referring to Eastern Oregon country.

"No, first time I have been in Oregon, but it looks like a place a feller could get used to. How long have you been here?"

"All my life." The winters are pretty cold but the grass is good and the people are good, so I couldn't ask for anything else. Craig has some stuff to do today so it will be just you and me. We will be stringing new wire and putting in a few rock jacks on a place I leased. Then I want to go check the cows that we moved over at the old Whitman place."

"Just point me in the direction and I will do the best I can," Charlie said as he stroked Flick's head.

25

Paige had gotten up early and was putting her final touches on her last design of the barn and corral layout. She was going to take it to her mother today, and she wanted it done before Abby got up. They were going out there to meet up with Samantha and Michael and get all the legal work laid out for the adoption and temporary foster care.

Paige had told Samantha they would come into town, but Samantha insisted that they would come out to Abe and Patricia's place. Besides it would give her a chance to see Piper and how Abby was getting along with him. It had been so long since she had visited with the Casons, Samantha was insistent about the location of the visit. Paige smiled and agreed.

Blue walked into Abby's bedroom, put one paw on the bed and whined. Abby rolled over, but she was not about to get out of bed. "No Blue," she mumbled. Blue took that as a sign and cautiously put her second foot up and dug at the bed. Abby sensed what Blue was doing and had to smile. The dog whined again and tried to wake the sleeping girl. Abby rolled away from the dog again as if sleeping. Blue stretched her nose as far as she could to reach, but Abby was still just out of reach. Blue took her hind leg and started to find the edge of the bed, knowing she was not supposed to be up there. She quietly and gently got her hind leg up and scooted closer to Abby. Blue touched her wet nose to Abby's ear and the girl couldn't take it any longer. She started to giggle, and Blue licked her cheek a couple of times then jumped off the bed and turned a couple of circles.

"Alright, alright, I'm up," she said as she folded the blankets back to get out of bed. Blue yipped at her in excitement, wiggling herself all over like a dog who had done her job well.

"You must have an alarm clock inside you. How do you know what time it is?"

Blue wiggled around again, then headed to the kitchen to check on Paige.

Paige got up and poured herself another cup of coffee. She had to grin as Blue pranced into the kitchen so proud of herself.

"Blue, you are a silly girl."

Blue wiggled around her leg and lifted her upper lip into a grin.

"You know you are."

Paige went back to the table and put her designs in her case. As she picked up the tablet, she glanced through the drawings and saw a glimpse of a horse head she had forgotten she had drawn a few weeks earlier. She thumbed through them again until she found it. A warm sensation went back through her body as her memory returned to that night. She thought of Craig Curry, and Paige could feel his hands on her heart. A sigh escaped her lips. She read the words under the picture one more time, *From the Heart*. She smiled as she closed the tablet and put away her colored pencils.

Abby came out and grabbed a packet of hot chocolate. She turned on the kettle to heat the water. Paige smiled at the possibility that they were going to be family and the fact that Abby had forgotten her crutch in the bedroom.

"Good morning," Paige said as she watched the young girl limp over to the cupboard to get a cup.

"Morning," Abby said as she returned to the stove, set down her cup, and waited. "That Blue. I swear she knows how to tell time," Abby said as she yawned.

Paige grinned. "Yeah, I think she does too. The problem is she keeps getting a little earlier every morning. Pretty soon she will be waking us up at four instead of six."

"No way am I getting up at four!" Abby said as if that would be the final straw.

"Well, I think she will be sleeping with you then, cause she usually doesn't take no for an answer," Paige chided.

The kettle started to sing and Abby lifted it from the stove and poured hot water for her chocolate.

"Paige, do you think this adoption thing will go through? I am kind of nervous about it. I don't know for sure what to expect."

"Well, to be honest, Abby, I don't know either. But let's just take this one day at a time and see how it plays out. I do know that I would be tickled to call you a sister or even family, but it is just a piece of paper. We already consider you family."

Abby looked at her for a moment and realized she did feel like family. "I never really thought of it like that, but I guess I kind of am, huh?"

"Yep." Paige grinned.

They sat and drank their drinks, then went out to do chores before they headed to Abe and Patricia's house.

***

When Paige and Abby pulled up in the Chevy pickup, they noticed a strange truck and trailer in the driveway parked next to the barn. "They must have company," Paige said. "Maybe a new horse to work."

Abby didn't say anything. Her mind was thinking that this might be her new home. Real home, one that she would come home from school to, where she would learn to drive and bring friends over, it was an odd feeling, yet exciting. It wasn't the home that she had had, and what kind of friends would she have? And school, that was coming up pretty quickly. What classes was she going to take? What kind of life was she going to live? A bit of panic struck her all at once. The dream of having a family, this was not her family. Her family was dead. She closed her eyes and took a breath. *One day at a time*, she thought. *One day at a time. They want me as family. They want me to be here.*

Paige looked at her. "Are you alright, Abbs?"

Abby looked back. "Yeah, I'm alright."

Patricia came out the front door with a smile on her face. "Hey girls, I have something to show you. Come out to the barn with me."

Paige and Abby both got out of the truck and followed her into the shade of the barn. There stood a buckskin mare. "Her name is Plaudit."

Abby had heard that name before. *What an odd name for a horse*, she thought. "Why do they call her that?" She couldn't remember why that name was so familiar.

"It is her granddad's name," Patricia explained as she leaned on the top of the rail. "So as not to forget where she came from, that is what Charlie calls her. She is going to foal any time. It will be nice to have a baby running around here for a little while."

"Who is Charlie?" Paige asked as she looked at the mare.

"He is a man who is working with Jim for a little while. We are going to house her until the foal is born, then he is heading up to Washington."

"She sure doesn't look like she feels very good."

"I am sure she doesn't. That baby has been kicking the heck out of her every time I come down here to check her," Patricia answered.

"What do you mean the baby is kicking her?" Abby asked as she stood and listened to Patricia and Paige as they talked.

Patricia looked over at Abby, then to the mare. "The foal has got to get in position to be born, and the bigger it gets, the harder it is for it to move around inside there. So if you watch you can see it move around."

"Really?"

"Yep, you did the same thing inside your mom before you were born, as did Paige before she was born. Sometimes I thought Paige kicked like a Missouri mule." Patricia grinned in memory.

Abby watched the mare's side and waited.

"Give it time. He might be sleeping," Patricia said as she watched Abby looking.

"How do you know it is a he?"

"I don't, just guessing."

"I think it is a girl," Abby said as she stared at the mare.

"We will find out in a day or so."

Samantha and Michael pulled up in the driveway in a brand new grey Mercedes. Paige had to smile.

"Is that them?" Abby asked.

"Yep, that is them," Paige answered as they headed back toward the house. She was excited to see Jonathon.

They greeted each other and Paige introduced Abby to Samantha. Paige peeked inside the carrier at Jonathon.

"He is so little." She reached in to touch his fingers, and his little hand gripped her finger. She couldn't imagine her hands ever being so small. He is beautiful, Samantha." Paige thought for a moment of Craig and losing his baby and wife.

Michael grabbed the diaper bag from the back and his brief case. He was on business while Samantha was here to visit.

"So you're the one who is riding Piper," Samantha said to Abby. "Do you like him?"

"I love him. I gave him a bath the other day and Abe let me lope him in the round pen."

Samantha smiled. It brought back a time when Abe lifted her onto Piper after the accident. The uncertainty and near panic she felt. She remembered how Abe coached her and how she carried that coaching into other areas of her life. "I remember the day he did that for me too," she said. "Probably a day I will never forget."

"Abe just picked me up and put me on him one day," Abby said.

"He did that to me too!" Samantha said. "Just like I was a feather, then he told me to breathe, like that was going to happen..." She laughed.

Abby liked her. "I know, he told me to feel Piper breathe underneath me, and I was so scared I couldn't feel anything there for a while."

They sat around the kitchen table and laid out papers and documents. Abe came in from riding a couple of colts and sat with them as they talked of old times and worked out details of the future. Abby got bored with all the technical talk and headed outside to see the horses. It had been over three hours and she wanted to see if she could see the baby kick inside the mother. She made it down to the barn and peeked in the stall where the new mare was. Lying in the sawdust was a newborn baby foal, still wet from birth. The mama was cleaning it. Abby watched as it tried to get up and fell down. Abby began to panic as the baby attempted to stand a second time and fell down on its nose. She turned back toward the house. Her legs felt numb and didn't seem to want to work. She couldn't move fast enough, so she began hollering.

"Abe! Patricia! There is something wrong with the baby horse!"

Abe was out the door and to the barn in a matter of seconds. Patricia and the rest followed in hot pursuit. Abe got to the stall and looked in to see a little buckskin filly learning to try and stand on wobbly legs.

"Is it crippled?" Abby asked as she watched the helpless baby bump her nose to the ground again.

Abe smiled. "No, she is just learning what her legs are for. Remember the other day when I asked you how long it took for you to learn to walk?"

"Why can't she stand?"

"Give her a little time. She will figure it out," Abe said. "She has to learn just like you did."

The mare continued to clean and lick on the baby as it tried to stand. It kept bumping and thumping around until, as everyone stood and watched, it found all four feet and stood wobbling back and forth. Plaudit was talking to it in soft murmuring nickers.

"I think Charlie will be happy," Abe said. "He has got a healthy mama and baby." He watched the baby nuzzle the front leg of its mom.

Abe picked up a pitchfork and quietly walked in to clean up the afterbirth. Abby watched him but didn't say anything. He put it in the wheelbarrow and grabbed a shovel. "Guess we could bring Shorty and Chance in for a while and let these two out in a couple of days. Give ole Plaudit here a chance to get some grass and give this baby a chance to figure out what her legs are for." He smiled at Paige.

Paige watched the baby nudge around on its mom. She thought of Libby and what it would be like to have a foal of her own. The baby had little black-tipped ears, black around both of her eyes, although her eyes were a hazel color, a black nose, and a line down her back along with a little black mane and tail, she was the spitting image of the Plaudit mare. Her whiskers around her mouth were fuzzy and long. She wobbled around picking up one foot and then the other trying to figure out which foot went where without falling. "You did good, mama. You did good," Paige whispered.

***

Charlie felt completely comfortable around Jim while they talked of different aspects of life as they drove out to do a little fence building. Jim grabbed a roll of barbed wire while Charlie grabbed a couple of wood fence stays to hold the wire. With fencing pliers in their hip pockets and staples in their shirts, they set out tacking up part of a downed fence. Flick stayed at Charlie's side as Charlie had promised. Jim was pleased to be able to take the man's word for it and admired the dog's loyalty to the soft words spoken by Charlie. Jim had brought one of his trusted saddle horses for Charlie to ride. Not knowing his riding ability, he wanted to get the job done without any incidents like Booger had displayed the day before. Charlie saddled the sorrel horse and stepped him around before stepping on with a saddlebag filled with smooth wire and fencing gear. They spent the afternoon riding the fence line tacking up wire and straightening up fence posts. They rode through the pasture for any lost pairs that might have been left behind the day before when Craig had helped move them. They loaded the horses and headed back to the Cason place that evening. All in all a good day's work.

When Jim pulled up, they both noticed a little buckskin baby standing in the paddock stall with Charlie's mare and they both grinned.

"Looks like you have a baby, Charlie."

Charlie's eyes welled up with the sight of the new baby trying to buck around her mama, still unsure of how her legs worked but giving it a try. *A new beginning,* he thought as he watched in silence for a moment before getting out of the truck.

26

After several attempts on Monday to get a hold of Paige, Craig was disheartened. Maybe she didn't want to see him again. He waited for her to call and got his things packed so all he would have to do when he left was throw it in the pickup.

He thought about going out to the Cason's but when he called to make sure they were home, there was no answer. He went out to the barnyard and looked at the horses. Cougar caught Craig's eye instantly, that golden colt stood out like a sore thumb in the pasture playing with the bay filly. He was as happy as he could be, showing no signs of the past dilemma of being chased by a mountain lion. He mischievously chewed on the filly's neck. Craig walked out to the mares grazing and brushed his hands along their backs. Cougar saw him and came loping up to see what was going on. He seemed to be excited about having a change in the routine.

"Hey, little buddy, how are you?" Craig asked as the colt came by to smell him. He touched his nose to Craig's hand then trotted away.

Craig looked toward the barn and knew if any time was right to teach giving in to pressure, it would be now. He decided to start to teach him to lead. So he walked to the barn, grabbed a can of grain, and called the mares into the corral.

"Come on, girls," Craig said as he shook the can of grain. Both mares heard the shaking of the grain and headed in at a trot. The babies followed in behind, bucking and kicking. The little bay filly was leery of walking into the corral. She seemed to notice the strange man standing at the gate as the mares came in. She hesitated and watched cautiously as her mom was caught, and she followed on the other side. Craig walked past the gate skimming the filly off into the round pen while her mom stayed on the outside of the corral. Craig tied her to the corral post. Cougar was bold and independent and was constantly looking for something to do. He boldly walked into the round pen.

Craig shut the gate then caught the second mare and tied her next to the first mare. The two babies stood inside of the corral. The mares seemed unconcerned with the fence between them. Craig went and got a bucket and sat in front of Cougar's mom. Cougar seemed unconcerned with where his mom was and explored around the round pen, chewing on the bay filly a couple of times.

All of the sudden, curiosity got the better of him. The guy on the bucket seemed to be interesting, so he wandered over to him. Craig sat there and let him explore a little. Cougar started nibbling on Craig, smelling his boots, his shirt, pulling at his hat. Craig just sat there and played with him a little. He got up from his bucket and walked around the pen leaving the little guy to his own. But Cougar didn't want to be ignored. He followed along seeing what his new toy human had going on. So Craig brought out his six-foot rope and started playing with it. Cougar watched him. Craig created a loop and played with it, then let the loop go. He scratched Cougar on the neck a couple of times. Then Craig brought the rope around his neck and pulled on it. Cougar felt the rope as it slid off his neck.

Craig walked away, but Cougar came at him again to see what he was up to. Craig again casually lifted the rope around Cougar's neck then created a little loop. He gave a little pull, then released the loop for the rope to fall away. About the fifth time, Cougar took a step toward the pressure of the rope, and Craig instantly released the pressure and the rope fell away again. The little game was fun and simple and the colt had no idea what he was doing. The bay filly watched from a distance for a while. Curious and not sensing any danger, she began to follow Cougar around while cautiously keeping Cougar between her and the man.

Craig, liking her curiosity, would stand at Cougar's shoulder with the young yellow colt as a barrier and would reach over and touch the filly on the shoulder for an instant. Then he'd return to working with Cougar. Pretty soon the filly liked the feeling of being scratched and rubbed, and the little rope that he draped on her didn't hurt at all. She soon fell into the game of who was going to get Craig's attention first. Craig would walk up, put the rope around the baby's neck, and the baby would feel the pressure and began to follow him. The rope would fall away each time after a couple of steps were taken. About thirty minutes later, Craig finished playing with the babies. He gave each of the mares another handful of grain then turned them loose back into the pasture. The introduction of the rope was a success. He smiled as he thought for a moment of how complete life was here. He stood there and watched the two colts nip at each other and let the silence sink into his heart. He didn't want to leave. He didn't want to go back to the empty apartment and listen to the busy world of busy people doing busy things.

He walked over to the haystack and grabbed two strands of hay string. He played with them for a moment thinking of a braid he used to do. He casually folded them in half, found the middle, then laid one over the other into a cross and started to braid them together into a square weave. He put one strand over the other and under and pulled tight. He kept his fingers moving and following through. When his twine would get short, he would splice in another twine and continue weaving until an hour later, he had a six-foot rope. Lost in the motion of braiding, Craig looked at his work and smiled. *Just like riding a bike*, he thought as he twisted and rolled it to get the braid right. He started on another twine and before he knew it, he had a set of reins made. He smiled as he inspected them, rolled them around, then just like it was nothing coiled them and hung them on a nail.

He spent the rest of the afternoon hammering loose nails in the corral rails and resetting a couple of posts. Booger came over and watched him dig out a posthole. He pawed at the loose dirt that Craig had taken out of the hole. "Hey, mister, don't do that," Craig said as he watched the horse's front foot destroy the little mound of dirt he wanted to put back in the hole. Craig reached out and touched the bay horse's shoulder. Booger looked at him for a moment then went back to smelling the dirt. Craig patted him on the neck a few times then went back to reshaping the hole before adding the new post and tamping it straight.

A little after four o'clock, Craig went to the house to start dinner. Spaghetti sounded fantastic, so he started to go through the cupboards. They were mainly empty. He thought for a moment, made a list of what he needed and headed into town for groceries.

As he pulled into the parking lot, he saw Toby walking out with a small bag of groceries and a case of beer.

"Hey, Tobe," Craig said as he walked toward the store.

"Hey, Craig, what are you doing tonight?"

"Gonna have dinner with my dad before I head back."

"Why don't you come over and have a beer with me?" Toby said as he put his groceries and the beer in the back of his Toyota pickup. He opened up the case, grabbed a couple of bottles and slipped them in the front seat.

"No, I am good, Toby. I think I am going to stick pretty close to home."

"Well if you change your mind, give me a call," Toby stated as he started to pop the top on one of the beer bottles.

"You be careful, Toby," Craig said as he passed.

"Awe it is only a couple of beers, Craig. It ain't gonna hurt me."

"It is your story. You can end it how you want," Craig replied.

Toby looked at Craig as he walked on past, then he looked at the beer in his hand. *My story…end it how I want?* He thought for a moment, *I can wait until I get home.* He put them back in the case in the back of the truck.

He watched Craig disappear into the store, then stepped into his little truck and headed home.

Craig roamed around the grocery store. What else could his dad use after Craig was gone? He grabbed some bread, butter, eggs, sugar, coffee, and before he knew it, his cart was full. He checked out and headed home.

As he started to unloaded the groceries, he heard the horses nicker in the corral. He glanced out across the barnyard. They were standing at the gate ready to be let out in the pasture.

His dad wasn't home yet, so he walked over and turned them out like he had seen his dad do so many times before. He hollered for the mares to bring them in their corral.

Then he went to work in the kitchen. He chopped up garlic, the sweet onion, and mushrooms and put them in a hot cast iron skillet. As they started sautéing, he added oregano, red pepper flakes, sweet basil, and salt, then turned it down to simmer. Then he started browning the meat in a separate pan. It felt good to be in the kitchen. He smiled to himself as he lifted the lid to the onions and mushrooms. The aroma wafted up and filled his senses.

Jim walked in the door just as Craig put the garlic bread in the oven. Jim was surprised at the aroma of fresh food in his home.

"What are you doing, Craig?" Jim asked as he walked into the house.

"Oh thought I would fix a little dinner for us tonight."

"Wow, what a treat. I didn't know you could cook like this. Man, this smells good."

Well this is what a city boy does when he can't think of other things to do." Craig smiled. "Actually, I used to cook with Lisa a lot and it kind of grew on me. I haven't done it since she died, but I thought tonight would be a good night to fix dinner, maybe have a beer on the porch. I wanted to do something special before I left."

"Boy, I sure can't argue with that," Jim said as he slapped his hands and rubbed them together. "This smells great!"

The evening was settling in. Craig looked out the kitchen window and saw the saddle horses grazing contently in the pasture. The brood mares were safely tucked away in the corral with their babies. It was a perfect evening. He looked up into the twilight and saw the North Star staring back at him. He felt Paige's hand on his chest over his heart. It felt so real he looked down and put his hand where hers had been.

What would Paige be doing now? He wondered. It didn't matter how busy he kept himself, she was always just a thought away. He lit up a couple of lanterns outside and set the table on the deck for dinner while Jim went in the bathroom to get washed up.

"Boy, Charlie is quite a hand," Jim said as he walked out of the bathroom. "I am pretty happy to have him help out."

"I kind of like him," Craig said as he took the food outside.

"He sure has a leggy buckskin filly. I can't wait to see her in a couple of weeks. He is talking like he might want to stay around here. I could sure use some help for a while."

They both sat down at the table and started dishing up their plates, talking of casual things through the evening.

27

Paige had gotten up early Monday and spent a couple hours on another set of plans for a park. *Four orders in one day. Well I guess that will keep my busy for a while.* The specs and the colors and texture were enough to make any sane person want to cry. But she tried to focus on one at a time and see where she would get before Abby got up. Michael had gotten right on the ball on Sunday and had all the papers drawn up for Paige and the adoption signed and notarized.

Paige spent the day in town attempting to get everything legally filed to be ready for the custody hearing and to proceed with the adoption on behalf of Abel Robert Cason and Patricia Marie Cason. Paige put all of her paper work in a folder in preparation for meeting with Ben in the morning.

She was late getting home that evening and it was almost twilight when she fed the horses. She locked them in for the night. Taking a few minutes for herself, she stood and listened to Libby's rhythmic chewing. Paige stood quietly stroking Libby's neck a couple of times as she glanced at the sky for a moment. The only star showing so far that evening was toward the North. That one star that stood the test of time was the same star that she could always look at and know he could see it too. She thought of Craig's tattoo and his story of finding his North. She felt his hand on her throat line and subconsciously reached her hand to straighten her necklace. *Make a wish* she thought, holding that feeling for a moment before heading to the house. Maybe she would call him. She didn't know what she would say, but she was sure she could think of something and she could talk while she made dinner. As she walked through the door, Blue trotted over, turned a couple of circles, whined then trotted down toward Abby's room. Paige followed.

Abby was sitting on her bed, her suitcase lying open with her clothes inside. She had taken her horse pictures down off the walls, and the room looked stripped and bare. Abby was trying to get her magazine horse pictures in her suitcase, but they were getting all messed up and crumpled.

Tears were running down her face. "I can't get these pictures to lay flat," she said, trying to hide the wetness on her cheeks. She took a few and attempted to straighten them with blurred vision. She sat still for a moment. "I can't do this." Silent tears became sobs as she looked up at Paige. "I just can't do this," she repeated as she cupped her face in her hands letting raw emotion of fear and loneliness torture her heart. Paige sat down and held her.

Two boxes of her belongings were on the floor and her one suitcase was all this young girl had to her name. An emptiness filled Paige as she remembered moving from the old place on Ruckles Creek so many years ago. She couldn't even fathom the thought of being ripped away from her parents to be shuffled around like an unwanted dog.

"We are going to get through this, Abby. One thing at a time, baby, one thing at a time." Paige started to tear up, but she blinked back the tears. "Let's focus on tonight, alright? We have done all of our homework and are gonna give ole Ben a run for his money."

Paige never picked up the phone.

***

Tuesday morning after chores were done, the mood was somber. *It is odd how one day can be blessings and the next filled with uncertainty,* Paige thought as she put the last of Abby's belongings in the back of the truck. *As one door closes, another opens,* she thought. The decision of that door was left in someone else's hands. She squared her shoulders as she crawled in and started the Chevy. Abby got in the passenger side.

Paige started to pull out of the driveway, and Abby looked over at her. "Are they going to take me?" she asked halfheartedly. She didn't want to leave the house. Looking in the rear view mirror, she felt that this might be the last time she would see this place that had begun to feel like home. A feeling of wanting to run away crossed her mind. If she ran now, she wouldn't have to deal with all this stuff. She could hide out some place and come back when things quieted down. Her mind was swimming with so many ideas. An unsure future gripped her mind. She was happy where she was and didn't want to sit in an office and have someone judge her, consider her helpless, or act like they knew what is best for her. Tears welled in her eyes as she let her imagination run wild.

Paige sensed the fear in the young girl's mind, "No, I don't think so, Abbs. We just have to do what they say, go through the evaluation and focus on today." Paige's voice was strong, and she looked at Abby. "We are going to give Ben a run for his money today, alright? We have done all that was required plus just a little bit more, Abby. We just have to play our cards."

Paige had all the recorded documents in her bag along with a letter from the attorney requesting that Abigail Sorenson be left to reside in her previous temporary foster home until proceedings of adoption had occurred.

They pulled into the parking lot, and Paige got the suitcase out of the back while Abby grabbed the two small boxes.

Abby remembered her last foster home the feeling of being lost, abandoned, so helpless and how stranded she felt until Paige walked through the door—a powerhouse of a woman who knew what she wanted. She remembered how she tried to get Paige to give up on her like the others had, but Paige didn't. A sense of strength filled Abby, and she straightened her shoulders and tried to walk like Paige.

The interview with Ben was rather short. He gave the documents a going over and then proceeded to read the letter. He looked over his glasses at Abby, then Paige.

"Well," he said with a sigh, "let's have you talk with Dr. Marks." His whiney voice had a tone of disgust. "Ms. Cason, if you will sit in the waiting room, we will call you in when we are done."

Paige got up and looked at Abby. "I will be right outside," Paige said as she nodded her head and straightened her posture. Abby did the same.

Paige sat in the waiting room that was sparsely furnished with hard chairs and laminate covered end tables. There was a magazine rack with numerous assortments of books and reading material filling the shelves. For thirty minutes, Paige flipped through magazines and read articles about how to have flawless skin. She looked at pictures of white couches sitting on white rugs. She thumbed through a magazine about family living, how to juggle Internet and TV for your children, and how computers help your children read. Perfect families with perfect smiles, she closed it. *This is family living?* She thought. If that was family living, she was doing everything wrong. She put the magazine down, took out a pad and pencil, and started to sketch.

Ben came out to the waiting room and called Paige through the door. Abby looked a little frazzled, Paige took a seat next to her. Ben followed Paige into the room, sat behind the desk, a barrier between real life on one side while judgment and control sat on the other. This was his domain. Beyond these walls, his life felt empty—an empty house with the Internet as his friend and TV shows as his lifestyle. But in this room, he thought he could control a situation to his specifications. He seemed not to appreciate Paige's complete work ethic, her inconsistent behavior on what he thought parents' responsibilities were. It seemed to have threatened his field of expertise.

He leaned back in his chair and folded his hands, looking at them in silence. He seemed to be milking his dominance of this situation for all it was worth. He had studied the papers, he had listened to the evaluation, and there were no errors he could find to hold this girl at this time. But he could make them squirm for a little while. In all actuality, he was happy to get this girl off his hands. She had been a problem since day one. He was happy that someone could handle her temper, and after this meeting it would be up to the judge. He leaned forward in his chair and looked over his glasses at Paige and Abby.

Paige shifted her gaze over to the doctor. Dr. Marks was a dark-haired man with a stern look and narrow shoulders. He looked like he held his shoulders up to make them broader, but all it did was make his neck look too short. He was seated to the right of Ben's desk and said nothing.

Ben took a breath and then began to speak. "On review of Abigail Sorenson, Dr. Marks and I have collaborated and have found that Abigail can remain in your household. But I want it understood, Ms. Cason, that if she misses another evaluation, I will have her pulled from your home and placed in another foster care facility until the adoption papers are completed." He took a breath. "Is that understood?"

"Yes, sir," Paige stated. "If you will give me the schedule, I will put in on my calendar."

"Well, talk to my secretary and have her give you the pending appointments. You may go."

Paige and Abby both got up and walked to the door. They grabbed Abby's belongings and walked to the secretary's desk. They waited patiently for her next few appointments and walked out of the office.

They returned Abby's things in the back of the pickup. Paige shut the tailgate and turned to look at her soon-to-be sister.

Without a thought, Abby wrapped her arms around Paige, grasping for a moment the strength that Paige had to offer. Abby felt tears run down her face. She couldn't stop them, but she didn't want to, she let them fall as she felt Paige's arms hold her. Abby allowed the feeling of warmth and love from this woman who had taken her in and made her family. It penetrated her heart.

Abby raised her head, "You're right," she sniffed. "We did give Ben a run for his money."

Paige grinned as she brushed the tears from Abby's cheeks, "Let's go home."

Home, Abby thought. Home had a new meaning, a depth she was just beginning to understand.

To celebrate Abby staying, Paige called John Greenly, Samantha and her family, and a couple other friends that Abby and Paige knew. She also wanted to call Jim and Craig. Her heart began to pound as she noticed the blinking light on the answering machine and the familiar phone number of Jim Curry. She hadn't checked it for the last couple of days, and she hadn't called Craig like she had anticipated the night before.

Paige didn't know what she would say, or even where she stood with Craig.

Paige pushed play. Craig had called three times on Sunday, twice on Monday, and again at nine thirty on Tuesday. This was what the latest message said.

"Came by to see you and noticed you were gone again. I am sorry, Paige, if I did something wrong. I'm getting ready to leave on Wednesday morning. Hope you are alright. Call me if you want to."

28

Tuesday morning Craig stretched himself awake. He went to the kitchen, started a pot of coffee, and grabbed the newspaper. He glanced through it real quick then prepared to go for a run. He jogged out past the horses and down the road. It was a great day for a run. An easy five miles would be sufficient, he thought, as he found his pace and let the rhythm carry him away. When he got home he jumped in the shower. He thought the run would take his mind off Paige, but she had settled in his heart like a weight on a fishing line. Maybe he should have done something differently. But it felt so right the other night... at least for him, but maybe not for her... He let the water run over him for a little while as he cleared his head. What was all this questioning? He would make one more attempt and then he had to let it go. *If she didn't want to see him that was going to have to be fine*, he mused.

He drove out to Paige's place. Again no one was home. He checked the horses, they were fed and all in their places, the troughs were all full, everything was well kept and clean. He was pretty frustrated. He went home more confused than anything. Maybe he really screwed up the other night, but nothing was making any sense. He dialed her number and left a final message. There was not much more to say about it. He attempted the Casons one more time and got Patricia on the phone.

"Hey, Patricia, are you guys going to be home today? I thought I would come out and say my goodbyes to you and Abe." He paused and listened. "Yep, I'm leaving first thing in the morning." He listened again. "Yes, I thought I could be out there in about a half hour." He didn't mention Paige nor did Patricia.

He jumped in his jeep and drove toward Haines. He loved this country, the snow-capped Blue Mountains with the Indian brave sleeping silently within the mountain folds. He noticed the Indian maid overlooking the valley, waiting for her love to wake. Craig took a deep breath and it smelled of fresh-cut hay that was being swathed in the hay field next to the road. A pickup passed him, and the driver waved. Craig waved back and wondered if he knew him. He had noticed that from around this county, people were usually friendly and would give a lending hand if they needed it. He turned on the road that went toward Anthony Lakes and continued. Not five minutes later, he pulled into the Casons' driveway.

Patricia was in the garden weeding. She had a bandana wrapped around her head and an apron wrapped around her narrow waist. She looked just like Paige, just a little older. Craig swallowed hard.

Patricia waved him over to the back door and asked him, "Would you like some iced tea?"

"That would be great," he said.

"Abe is in the barn. Do you want to go see Charlie's filly? She is a dandy."

"Thanks," he said. "So she had it, huh?"

"Yep and Abby was here to watch her stand for the first time too. It was a beautiful thing."

"It sure has been great being back here for a while," Craig stated trying to maintain composure of leaving.

"It sure was great having you home, Craig. It seemed like you came home just in time for all the excitement."

"Yeah, there was plenty of that for a few days, wasn't there?"

"Oh, but it is only just beginning," Patricia answered.

"What do you mean?" Craig asked confused. "What is going on?"

"Well," she beamed," Abe and I are looking into adopting Abby."

"Really?" He was surprised. "How did that come about?" he asked looking confused about Paige and all that was said a few nights ago.

Patricia thought for a moment. She then started the story from Sunday morning and Abby possibly being sent away to a school for troubled kids.

Craig cringed. "No!" he said before he could stop himself.

"That is what Paige said." Patricia continued sketching out the last few days and ending with the appointment this morning. "We haven't heard, but we are hopeful that Abby can stay with Paige until the hearing."

Craig started putting the pieces together and saw how everything rolled together. "Boy, she wasn't lying when she said her life was full," he said out loud, not thinking about it.

"It has been over full, for months now," Patricia added.

As they walked into the barn Abe saw him and said, "Hey, Craig, hear you are getting ready to leave back to the big city."

"Yah, I am flying out tomorrow," Craig said halfheartedly.

"Come and take a look at Charlie's filly. That Plaudit mare sure threw a pretty baby."

They walked out to Shorty's pasture. There was a little spindly buckskin filly, bucking and attempting to play around the mare. "Charlie wants to call her Pistol Annie. I think it sounds pretty cute. We will see when he fills out the papers."

"Boy, she is a cutie, Abe." Craig watched her play, her little black-tipped ears pinned back as she started to run around her mom. Her legs kept getting in her way as she attempted to lope around. "I bet Charlie is thrilled."

"Yeah, he is pretty happy and sure seems to enjoy working with Jim," Abe stated as he watched the baby.

"Boy, give her a week and old Cougar will have some competition."

Abe smiled. "Well, she is off to a good start."

All three headed back to the house and sat on the porch. Patricia poured them some lemonade.

"So," Abe said as he placed his elbows on the table, "you are headed back to the big city."

"Well, Mr. Cason," Craig looked at him and kind of grinned. "I am kind of at a crossroads, I guess." Craig was surprised at his own honesty.

Abe looked across the table at Craig. "What do you mean, bud."

"I had a life in New York, but I wouldn't say it was a real life. I have been on the police force for four years now and I don't like my job much." He sighed. "I think I want to come home," he took a breath, "and I think I have fallen in love with your daughter." Craig couldn't believe what he had just said, the reality of truth was sinking in, but there was some anxiety in his heart as he continued. "But I don't know if she is going to want me, I guess."

Abe and Patricia were silent. Then Abe said, "Have you told Paige this?"

"No, sir, actually I hadn't even told myself until just now." He kind of grinned, then got serious again. "I know I am a widower. I have seen some pretty ugly things in my life, but, Mr. Cason, your daughter brings out the beauty in everything I see."

"Well, I think you are going to have to tell her that. We sure can't choose for her. But if you are asking for my blessing, you have it, Craig."

"I think I am coming home. This is where I belong." Craig breathed a sigh of relief.

The phone rang and Patricia answered it.

"Hey Mom, it is me. Do you and Dad want to come over tonight and celebrate? Abby is staying with me until the hearing!" Paige was close to tears.

"Oh, honey, that is great."

"I was trying to get ahold of the Currys and see if they wanted to have a barbeque with us."

"Hold on, Paige, I will let you ask Craig. He is right here." Patricia handed the phone to Craig and smiled.

Patricia reached for Abe and said, "She has custody until the hearing." He stood up wrapped his arms around her and held his wife.

Craig took the phone. "Hello?" he said.

Just hearing his voice made Paige almost panic. She couldn't believe how much she missed him. Her heart started beating in her throat. She had so much she wanted to say but didn't know where to begin.

"Craig? I just tried to call your house. I wanted to say I am sorry I missed your calls. Things have been absolutely crazy," Paige rambled to get everything out in one breath. "But it seems like it is all working out pretty well. I wanted to invite you and Jim over for a barbeque to celebrate. I get to keep Abby with me until the adoption goes through. I mean Mom and Dad are trying to adopt Abby, and we have all the paperwork done…I really don't know where to begin…There is so much I want to tell you." Paige paused to clear her thoughts and maybe attempt to make a little more sense of her rambling. She listened. There was no sound on the other end. *Did the line go dead?* She wondered. "Craig? Are you there?"

Craig felt his throat close up while tears welled up in the corner of his eyes when he heard her smooth familiar voice on the other end of the phone. He swallowed hard as he tried to pay attention to what Paige was saying. He cleared his throat a little. "I am here," he said, his voice a little choppy. "I am right here."

FROM THE HEART

BOOK III in

UNSPOKEN SERIES

A.K. MOSS

Craig rolled over. He could feel Paige next to him.

"I am glad you are here. I missed you," he whispered. He wanted to open his eyes, but something told him not to.

He waited for a reply. He prayed for one, just one word from her lips, but only silence. He reached over to wrap his arms around her to pull her to him. All he felt was a pillow. He pulled it to his chest and held it. He heard the cars outside in all the busyness. New York… home…a world away from the world he loved.

60954081R00181

Made in the USA
Charleston, SC
07 September 2016